COMPLETENESS *of the Soul*:
The Life and Opinions
of
JAY BREEZE,
ROCK STAR

To: Jim

Hope you'll enjoy!

Best,
Jim Bow

COMPLETENESS *of the Soul*:
The Life and Opinions
of
JAY BREEZE,
ROCK STAR

Edited and Arranged by His Friend,
Charles D. Beagle

Assisted by
Jim Booth

Best Wishes Jim Booth

Queen's Ferry Press

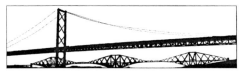

Queen's Ferry Press
8240 Preston Road
Suite 125-151
Plano, TX 75024
www.queensferrypress.com

Copyright © 2012 by Jim Booth

Published 2012 by Queen's Ferry Press

Cover photo courtesy of Lea Booth

First edition August 2012

ISBN 978-0-983907-18-3

Printed in the United States of America

Praise for COMPLETENESS *of the Soul*:

"Jim seems to have found a unique way to illuminate the interior voice of fame. A way to convey the restless, active, eternally adolescent mind of an aging rock star. A way to convey the pros and cons of walking the tightrope of celebrity while offering an accurate glimpse into the heart of that life."

—**Don Dixon**, record producer (R.E.M., The Smithereens, Marshall Crenshaw, Marti Jones), composer, performer (Arrogance, Don Dixon and the Jump Rabbits)

"Jay's story is told primarily through his collected letters and journal entries, a form that lends itself to honesty and raw emotion. Jay is a lover of literature, a lover of rock 'n' roll, and a man who wants to quote Keats and Elvis Costello in the same sentence. His writing alternately poignant and humorous, he simultaneously damns and embraces his fame while hanging from Shakespearean banisters."

—**Teresa Milbrodt**, author of *Bearded Women: Stories*

For Everybody's Angels . . .

Epigraphs

"The past is not dead. In fact, it's not even past."
—William Faulkner

"When the many are reduced to the one, to what is the one reduced?"
—Zen Koan

"They're boys with guitars and dreams. . . ."
—Hatter/Breeze

AU LECTEUR

Dear Reader:

You're owed better. I'm a writer—a journalist, really. I'm no poet. And this calls for a poet—or at least a damned good lyricist. I have to say these things some time, and I guess that time is now. We love our friends. We support them and we do our best for them—or we try to. We might call these our duties.

My duty here is to try to do my best for a friend. Since, as Robert E. Lee observed, duty is the "sublimest" word in the English language, I should feel honored and pleased to introduce this collection of writings by my friend, the rock star Jay Breeze.

But I don't. Instead I feel cheated. Cheated and pissed and bewildered—the way I always feel when I see pointless waste.

My friend is dead. A guy who drank gallons of intoxicants and ingested pounds of medications (both legal and illegal) and otherwise regularly engaged in reckless self-endangerment loses control of his car driving home, sober, from my house in a minor snowfall, and hits a tree.

He'd finally settled himself and made peace with losing the love of his life. He'd begun to develop a sense of himself as a person beyond his rock star status. He'd made it through the glitz and bullshit and was on his way to being just Jay Brent again. He was finally starting to be happy . . . a little. . . .

And he hits a frigging tree.
Pointless waste . . .

It's impossible to summarize people, of course. That's the problem with Jay—he's been summarized way too often and not very accurately. Then, too, any summary could only tell you things you probably already know: Jay Breeze, nee Brent, was a member of the rock group called The Lost Generation. Most rock critics, including this one, consider them one of the best four or five bands to emerge in the 1970s. As a result of being so good, they got rich and famous. Less the typical '70s arena rock heroes like Led Zeppelin or The Doobie Brothers and more like their brethren from the '60s, they took power pop, as it's now called, several steps forward. They released nine albums, seven of which went platinum, the other two gold. (Update: the last two albums, in the years since the group's "retirement," have now gone platinum.) Like their heroes, The Beatles, they believed in and were good at writing melodic rock songs.

Those songs—"Mary, Quite Contrary," "Masquerade for Two," "Never Stop," "Her Smile, Winter 1974," "Loss of Control," and my favorite, "Leaves Like Love on Fire." If you've listened to rock radio between 1974 and the present, you know these songs. You most likely know all the words.

Jay Breeze wrote those words.

I'm reminded suddenly of an interview with Bob Dylan. In the interview he complained that people often approached him because of some song he'd written. He adamantly disavowed responsibility toward any fan: "Just because I write some song he thinks is about his life don't give him the right to come bothering me," Dylan said.

How different Jay was. I spent a lot of time with him after he came back to Chapel Hill once the band retired. He wanted to finish his undergrad degree and work on an MFA in creative writing—do some "real writing," he'd say (as if writing song lyrics that millions can recite was somehow worthless). Wherever we went during our weekend rambles, whether to a local restaurant or posh resort (his treat always—"Charlie, I'm a multi-millionaire," he'd respond to my occasional protests), a steady stream of people accosted him. Jay was unfailingly polite, signing sometimes a dozen or more autographs. I asked him why he didn't avoid the hassle—he certainly was rich enough for handlers.

"Charlie," he said softly, his face sad even when he smiled, which he seldom did once he became famous, "these people made me. They've bought my records. They've gone to my concerts. I'm theirs."

"Like Dr. Frankenstein made his monster," I said, smiling cynically.

"Yeah—I guess you're right." He looked away shyly as he often did. "The monster never could get a break, could it?" he asked, turning to me, his eyes full of a question for which I had no answer.

I shivered as if someone had walked across my grave. "Be careful, Jay," I said.

I've always felt it wasn't enough.

Jay wanted to be a writer—he wrote off and on all the time he was in Lost Generation. Once he came back to UNC he tried hard to write. I'm not sure how much success he had. I never expected he'd go so far as to name me as his literary executor. I didn't know he'd even prepared a will. . . .

There were lots of papers in his estate, but most were either unfinished ideas or pedestrian stuff I knew he'd not want published. I found exactly one useable short story which I've included below. Finally it occurred to me to check his laptop where he kept, as he called it, "all my favorite crap." That's where I found the stuff you'll read below. I vaguely remember seeing a few of the things I've edited into the "Book of Days." I never knew about the letters to Angel until I found them on his computer.

Check that. I think maybe Jay hinted to me about these letters.

Shortly after Angel's death, just before he left for that ill-advised winter tour that ended abruptly in San Francisco with Mick Norris's broken hand and our friend Ralph Dodge's death in a plane crash, Jay stopped by my office at the journalism school to ask a crazy question. In those sad days he often did that. Anyway, what Jay asked was something like, "Charlie, do you think the dead can read?"

"Damn, Jay. I never thought about it," I remember saying. "Why?" I felt he wanted to talk about Angel and I hoped to get him to. If I could tell you one thing about Jay from my friendship with him, it would be that his greatest asset and his greatest liability as a friend were one and the same: his reticence. You could tell Jay anything and know that he would never repeat it. He had the trust of many and never betrayed a soul.

Of course, he never betrayed himself, either. He never opened any of those doors into himself that we all need to open on occasion to maintain our mental and spiritual health. Jay just kept it all in. Maybe that explains the alcohol and occasional drug problems.

Anyway, he never talked. Well, not to me. He talked to Angel—as these letters will attest. He told her everything, I think. Maybe that's the definition of love. His, anyway . . .

I could launch into a long recital of the debate that went on about whether or not these letters should become public. Since you're reading this book, you know where I stand.

If you're feeling ambivalence, I'll offer you the question that convinced all the relevant people (Jay's parents and brother, Angel's parents, Teddy, Mick, Sid, and me) to go ahead with this: "Shouldn't we let Jay speak for himself?"

I had this brilliant plan when I started this introductory letter. I was going to use Baudelaire's "Au Lecteur" as a gloss. Baudelaire's poem, for those of you who don't know it (shame on you), is an indictment. After a powerful, sinister, and inclusive description of both writer and audience (I offer the English translation with a "get the fuck over it" for purists who expect the French):

Stupidity, delusion, selfishness, and lust
Torment our bodies and possess our minds,
And we sustain our affable remorse
The way a beggar nourishes his lice.

The poet goes on to catalog the possibilities of vice and our gradual decline into it. After exploring the seven deadly sins and some other, more exotic ones (gotta love that Baudelaire), the poet points to the greatest monster of all, Boredom, of whom he says, "You know this squeamish monster well/—hypocrite reader, —my alias, —my twin!"

I'm guessing you don't get it. No, you have nothing to do with it—a rock star dies, you hear his songs played intensely for a day or two, then something else happens and you move on. There are plenty of other rock stars and plenty of other songs. Off he goes to the dustbin of history, his role played out.

What is it Jagger says about the singer and the song? Or Henley (via Yeats) about the dancer and the dance? Or Breeze in "Boys With Guitars and Dreams"?

> See them struggle—
> See them make it—
> Sometimes see them fly;
> Watch them stumble—
> Watch them fall down—
> Sometimes watch them die. . . .
>
> You can't separate them. They're all one.
> We're all one.
> You, Jay, me.
> Reader—alias—twin . . .
> Face the music.

Charlie Beagle

Fins

Dear Angel,

What can I tell you about these dreams? They come and come. I stay up as late as I can, but I have to sleep.

Usually they begin this way: We are at the Sunset Grille—me on the barstool nearest the poster of us from the "Anthems for Doomed Youth" tour, you on the stool next to me, the others scattered around us in carefully studied disarray. Sometimes Sid sits next to you, sometimes Mick. Always Teddy leans against the wall, his face half-hidden by a cloud of cigarette smoke. Next to him is always the second-prettiest woman in the place. Just my opinion . . .

Late, usually about two, Andrew will turn off the jukebox and pull out the guitar. Sometimes Teddy plays, sometimes Mick. I always sing.

We usually start with several we haven't recorded yet to weed out the sunshine fans. When only fanatics are left we'll do a couple of tunes we know they'll love: If Teddy has the guitar it'll be a slow, bluesy, acoustic version of something like "Loss of Control" or "Salad Days." If Mick's playing it'll be romantic and folksy like "Her Smile, Winter 1974" or "Leaves Like Love on Fire."

As "Her Smile" ends I'll turn to you and you'll smile as you always do. If it's "Leaves" you'll look over at me and there'll be a tear on my cheek that no one else but you can see.

And you'll reach over and catch the teardrop on your finger and touch it to your lips, then to mine. And we don't have to say it because it's so much so. And then everything dissolves the way things do when they're too real to be anything but dreams. . . .

. . . Then we are standing on the beach. Clouds skulk over the water; waves slap the shore almost maliciously. Things look cold, forbidding, but instead it's muggy; my shirt clings to my chest, billowing behind me as the wind off the ocean hits us. Our hair is intertangled. The earring in my left lobe jangles, the gold guitar swinging against the loop from which it hangs. You turn to me as if you hear it. "Do you want to swim?" you ask.

I nod and peel my shirt over my head. It catches on the earring and I have to work it loose. By the time I do you have shed your own shirt and begun walking to the breakers. "C'mon, Jay," you call. Your words hit me like the wind. I start after you. The straps of your swimsuit are a moving X as you swing your shoulders and move ahead.

You stop at the water's edge and I catch up to you. A wave washes over our feet. The tide is coming in. The ocean is tepid, old-bathwater warm. The North Carolina coast in July. I turn to you to say something about the water temperature but your eyes are fixed on the horizon. Your face in profile is beautiful and soft, your eyelashes longer than most memories.

Your hair—between blonde and golden—indescribable, I realize—reaches your shoulders. Mine is almost as long. Can you detect a rock star in this picture? I stupidly told you once that you looked like a German girl I had a thing with during the '76

European tour. You were unmoved.

Impulsively I run into the waves and dive. When I come up I swim straight toward the horizon. The bottom drops away quickly, from knee to waist to shoulder depth. I stop out of fear. I almost drowned one night when I jumped off some boat in south Florida during a party when I was out of control back in '79. It might have been Buffet's boat. Maybe one of the Eagles was there. I don't remember. I'm not sure. It's all vague and indistinct.

I turn and watch you wade casually into the water. When it reaches your waist, you lower yourself and let a breaker sweep over your head. You stand, streaming, and push your hair back. You say something, but I cannot make it out. I turn and duck beneath a wave. When I come up, facing you, your voice reaches me. All I can make out is "back."

I look down the beach. The public fishing pier is indistinct, as if it might disappear in the low clouds. A line for a song comes to me: "An indistinct vision in a marginal landscape." Then another, maybe better one: "An indistinct day in a marginal life."

Teddy would love that. Well, damn Teddy Hatter. Damn The Lost Generation. Damn money. Damn rock-and-roll.

You shriek, then fall silent. I look at you, my body barely moving. You are absolutely still. You stare at the water perhaps fifteen feet from us.

There is a shark. It is big, at least five feet long, maybe bigger. It moves casually through the space between us, undulating marginally. A blue-gray shadow. As it reaches us, its fin breaks the water briefly, vaguely.

We both remain still.

The fish continues down the beach toward the pier. Soon it has disappeared.

Once it is out of sight, you walk deliberately toward me and reach out. I cannot seem to move, so you plunge your hand into the sea and slide your fingers down my arm until they grasp my hand. You tug and I stumble after you.

Then we are standing on the shore. Suddenly your weight sags against me. I brace myself and cling to you. Your arms move upward in slow motion and curl about my neck. We stand, adhering, your damp hair tickling my chest. You twist your head back and kiss my Adam's apple. . . .

What do you think, Angel? This is the one I have over and over. I asked Charlie Beagle about it. As usual, he listened carefully, then got up from his chair and walked out of his office. I followed him down the hall. "Let's take a walk across campus and smoke a cigarette," he said.

We walked for about an hour. It was just getting dark. Charlie never said a word. Finally we stopped at the bell tower. Charlie turned to me. "Jay, be careful. It's love. I'll see you. I have a night class." Then he walked away, into the darkness.

Just like him.

I miss you. I wish there were some way, you know? Beside the dreams, I mean. And these letters, of course. The letters are more for me, I think. I feel that everything I tell you is stuff you already know.

The dreams. The dreams. When I first started having them, I thought they were just a reaction. You know, you're working through something that's maybe the most significant change in your life, and it sort of takes you over for a while. It hovers about your consciousness when you're awake, messing with you while you're trying to do all the usual stuff. And when you sleep (if you can—you know how I struggle) it bubbles up. That's what I thought for a while. Now I'm not so sure. It's about messages, I think. Messages—from you to me, me to you, me to myself.

Here's another dream I had about a week ago. It was the only one that night. I'd stayed up until four because I kept hearing your voice as I'd start to doze off, so I'd get up and walk around the hotel looking for you. Finally I piled a bunch of pillows on the floor in front of the television and watched *The Sandpiper* with Richard Burton and Elizabeth Taylor until I fell asleep. Then I dreamt this . . .

. . . No one is allowed on the pier without shoes, so we go back to the car and put on our sandals. Through the bait shop/restaurant/souvenir shop then out onto the pier. We make our way toward the horizon, the beach dropping away below and behind us, the ocean stretching out ahead.

Some of the planks are rotting. The owners of the pier are dealing with this danger. *STROLL AT YOUR OWN RISK* say prominently posted signs. One must step carefully or plunge thirty feet into the sea.

The proximity of calamity. A regular feature of my life.

I shiver, perhaps due to a breeze that strikes me unprepared, possibly for some other, indistinct reason. You clutch my arm. "Did someone just walk across your grave?" you ask.

Farther out, the pier is made of all-new lumber. Some hurricane has blown away most of the old pier.

There are many fishermen. They are catching sharks. Baby sharks. The pier is littered with carcasses—some gray, some blue, some indistinct.

I realize I don't know my sharks as well as I should. Never have.

Their little fins make accidental designs behind the fishermen. Some of them lie on their anterior sides with their dorsals sticking up. They look like illustrations in some perverse children's book. Little sharkeys swimming down the pier.

You step over to one of the sharks that's still twitching from a deathblow indifferently delivered by a grizzled fisherman with a stick he keeps propped against his folding stool. You move your foot close to the fish to nudge it.

"Better not do that, missy," rasps the fisherman. "Little sumbitch will take part of your toe off."

You jerk your foot away and turn to me for protection.

I look at the baby sharks then and I see people at record company parties. I start to laugh. Soon I can't stop.

Abruptly you brush past me and run back down the pier and toward the beach. I run after you, keeping my eyes on your back, never looking down at the rotting planks. "Faster, faster/The lights are turning red. . . ."

I suppose I could go see another shrink and get him/her/it to do a dream analysis and tell me what the hell all of this means. But you know how I am about psychology. It's all bullshit. As I've told you several times, the only one who can fix me is me.

I wonder why I think I need fixing. Here's one last dream . . .

 . . . The restaurant is not crowded, just busy. We are lucky and get a table looking out on the Cape Fear

River. What was breeze is now wind; the lights along the docks sway, and farther out ship lights bob toward and away from us in weird geometric patterns. It starts to rain, and big drops flatten themselves against the glass like fans against a limo window, smearing into one another, rendering the light and themselves incoherent.

The waiter is obsequious. He has recognized me. Instead of admitting the fact so we can deal with it openly, he's decided to grant me my "privacy" and subtly grovel. When he gets back to the kitchen his mouth will work like that of the gasping little shark on the pier this afternoon. Sumbitch will take part of my soul off if I'm not careful.

We order drinks and an appetizer. He's gone. In a couple of minutes I see the restaurant manager heading for our table. He's my age, maybe a little older. A fan for sure. He'll know the words to the songs, the album titles, everything. And he'll want to tell my life to me as if it's history.

"They know who you are, don't they?" you ask in a tone that suggests I've committed a crime by being famous. I nod. Guilty.

The waiter passes the manager who has been stopped by some locals. He sets drinks before us. I hold up my hand as he turns to leave and knock back the scotch and soda. The scotch is cheap, and there's too much soda in the drink.

"Again," I say as I hand him the glass. "And this time, tell the bartender not to use the well scotch. Use the good stuff. And make it a double."

He bows, of all the things for a waiter in a seafood joint in Southport, NC, to do, and hustles off.

Just before the manager arrives, you reach across

the table to me. I don't move my hand, so you take it in yours and squeeze. "You don't have to," you say softly.

"Rule #1: Once a Rock Star, always a Rock Star." I smile, but the look in my eyes is so hard that you shiver. "Somebody walk on your grave?" I ask facetiously.

You turn and look out the window, even though you can't see anything except indistinct shapes because of the rain and wind. I think that, for once, you might actually cry.

The manager/fan is here. "Excuse me," he says as a mannerly way of invading the privacy that his establishment seemed so set on protecting. "Are you Jay Breeze?"

"My name is Jay Brent," I say flatly.

"That's your real name, right? But you are Jay Breeze. Of The Lost Generation. You and Teddy Hatter and Mick Norris and Sid Vegas."

He smiles, pleased mightily with himself. Now he'll give me a discography and tell me which is his favorite and ask why the band broke up.

And he does. He reels off titles, not so much for me, but for his own satisfaction. "*How Do You Like Your Blue-Eyed Boys?*, *Anthems for Doomed Youth*, *War and Peace and Boredom*, *We Are All a*— What do you guys call that album?"

"THE Lost Generation," I say, watching you. *We Are All THE Lost Generation.*"

"Oh, man, that's it. You all were fantastic. After Led Zep you're my favorite group. I think 'Loss of Control' is as good a song as anyone ever did." He's beside himself. I'm going to have to sign a bunch of autographs for his family and friends.

"Thanks."

I never know what else to say. The waiter returns with my drink. I pluck it from his tray and take a big gulp, then set the glass down and stare at it.

The manager's voice says in a confidential tone, "Hey, dinner's on the house. Order anything you like. I recommend the soft-shell crabs."

He motions for the waiter to freshen our drinks. Simultaneously, we put our hands over our glasses. We smile subtly at each other.

I look up at the fan club. They're standing beside me, hovering. They'd be circling if they could. Jimmy Buffett's boat comes to mind and I get a vague insight into why I jumped overboard. Then I think of those damned little sharks swimming down the pier.

"Fins to the left, fins to the right . . ." I sing softly.

You join in with, "And you're the only game in town. . . ."

This stuff really happened, didn't it? The weekend that we went down so I could meet your parents. I wish they didn't think I'm such a bad person. If they'd talk with me, it would help.

Nevermind. It does no good to go over things again and again.

So much of everything is a dream, Angel. Maybe, as Calderon says, everything.

I'm scared without you, you know?

And I have these dreams. They come and come.

Sometimes it seems that dreams and memories are the same things.

Do I wake or sleep?

Love,
Jay

(Editor's Note: These are some of the "Day Book" writings of Jay Breeze, who was, as most of you know, the bassist and lead singer of the band The Lost Generation. [As you read you'll recognize the names of the other members of the band—Sid Vegas, Mick Norris, and, of course, Teddy Hatter.] As many of you also know, Jay died in December of 1992 when he crashed his vintage 1962 Corvette into a tree while driving in a snowstorm. So, yeah, in some ways he was your typical rock star.

I knew Jay from the time we were fifteen, nearly twenty-five years. He was a great guy who made great music and spent his whole adult life thinking he never did a damned thing artistically worthwhile. I found these observations, aphorisms, musings, and private jokes in one of those "write your own" blank books as I examined the contents of Jay's knapsack one afternoon shortly after I learned I was his literary executor. I couldn't figure out what to do with the stuff. Finally, it occurred to me that I could publish it here between letters. You're on your own from there.)

JAY'S BOOK OF DAYS

All our lives we remember moments that would seem trivial to anyone but ourselves. Is this our uniqueness?

I think of you several times each day; only my discipline keeps me from thinking of you more.

So much trouble to get into, so little time!

All the autumn afternoon I read poetry and tried to realize how people are separate.

Some notion of life through music . . .

How could Mozart lift his heart so high?

Does anything matter but love?

To understand life through the objects of the world: a book, a comfortable chair.

Sometimes life feels close-fitting, like a shirt shrunk from washing.

Perhaps you are asleep as I write this.

Sometimes it's a rattle in your soul that you try to fix by tightening the screws on yourself or something equally stupid.

Drugs and alcohol are bad for you, they say—but they

seem to be pretty good for me.

Sometimes happiness is simply looking at her.

Too much of what we think is what other people tell us we should think.

Grace is sometimes a matter of luck.

I used to think the world was crazy . . . now I realize it's me.

We Are the Lost Generation

September 21, 1991

Dear Angel,

You know, you have that thing you say to me
—you say, "Hey, whaddya doin'?"

Here's what I've been doing for the last twenty
years . . .

I was born and brought up in Reidsville, North
Carolina. Reidsville's a town of about twenty
thousand up close to the VA/NC border. It's only
about ten miles from Eden, where Teddy Hatter and
Charlie Beagle grew up.

Teddy and Charlie were acquaintances of mine
before we all went to UNC together. Actually, that's
not quite true. Teddy and I were acquaintances;
Charlie and I were friends. We knew each other from
literary competitions that were held for all the high
schools in the county. It was through Charlie that I
met Teddy.

Charlie (you insist on calling him Professor
Beagle) used to get me to come over and listen to his
and Teddy's band rehearsals. I always thought their
band had a cool name—Nothing Sacred. Maybe I
knew even then that it would be Teddy and me in a
band. I remember that each time I went to hear them
(I tried not to go too often even though they rehearsed
three times a week—you know me, Angel, the soul of
modesty) Teddy would get me to sing a song with
them. He kinda flipped out when I sang one I'd

written for them. He went right to work on it, embellishing and changing until it was half his own. I revised a couple of lines to fit the rhythm changes he'd made and we'd written our first song together. Took us maybe twenty minutes.

The song was "Her Smile, Winter 1974." We kept changing the year until we finally recorded it in the fall of 1975. It was a top-ten hit for us in the winter of 1976. The reason it's called "Her Smile, Winter 1974" instead of "1975" is that somebody wrote down the song title for the record company (Teddy or Mick, I think—does it matter?) from an old song list and we hadn't changed the year.

This isn't telling you much, is it?
What would you like to know?
I'd tell you anything.
I love you, you know.

Well. We all graduated high school in 1970. Teddy went to NC State, Charlie and I to UNC. That's not quite true. Teddy spent most of his time in Chapel Hill with us, so he was only nominally an NC State student.

He was really a rock musician. That was all Teddy ever wanted to be. He lived and breathed it. He still does. Oh. He transferred over to UNC after a semester. How the hell he got in I'll never know. I can't imagine he passed a single course he was taking at NCSU. I think, though he never has said, that he withdrew about midterm of that first semester and applied for some kind of special admission to UNC. Anyway, come January of '71, he was with us.

Charlie was a different case. He went for the

books. Big time. College was Charlie's thing. He still hung around and all that, but he was mainly into his studies. He wanted to be a journalist. Actually, he wanted to be like Hunter Thompson, "only with more self-control," he said.

And that's where I came in. Charlie lost interest in the band.

He and Teddy had found Mick right after arriving in Chapel Hill. They then went through a series of drummers.

I don't know what it is about drummers, Angel. They're probably the most vital part of any band—the heartbeat, you know? And yet, they're always the least stable guys, the ones most likely to disappear without a trace. Anyway, there were at least half a dozen in quick succession. Then Sid showed up when the guys were opening for somebody or other at Town Hall, the favorite college club in Chapel Hill. I was working as their roadie and saw the whole thing.

Sid just walked up to the stage after their set and said, "You guys write great songs, but you need a drummer. I'm him." Interestingly, their drummer at the time was packing up his kit and heard Sid. He came over and got in Sid's face big time. Sid invited him outside to fight. The drummer backed off.

At that point Teddy looked at Charlie, Charlie looked at Teddy, and in the same breath they both told the drummer he was fired. Charlie told me later it was a no-brainer. If Sid was crazy enough to fight somebody for the job, he was the man for them.

Boy, I do go on, don't I?
Thanks for letting me tell all this.
I still haven't told you much.

Sometimes I think, what's there to tell?

Sid joined up in mid-October of 1970. That was really the last time Charlie and Teddy acted as a united front. I'd never felt like I could get past that— in terms of the band, I mean. We were all friends and all that, but there was this deeper connection between them that I always felt uneasy trying to breach. You understand how it is—you sense two people know something that you can never know, and no matter how close you get to them you'll never have that thing they have.

Kind of like us, I guess.

Anyway, from that point in mid-October when Sid joined, things just kind of went on the skids between Teddy and Charlie. Charlie took to hanging out with some J-school types and Teddy started spending all his time with Mick and me—and Sid.

Usually guys leave bands over women. You know, somebody gets a girlfriend and pays more attention to her than to the band and pretty soon he gets himself thrown out. So he consoles himself that he made the better choice—you know, love over music. But I doubt that anyone who ever left the music for a person was ever really satisfied. But Charlie left over wanting to be a writer rather than play music. I've often admired him for that. And I've always been troubled by it because I could never figure out why I didn't. That's why I'm back in school now.

The music is bigger than anyone, Angel.
That's how it is.

And you can try to leave it, but it will never leave you.

Yeah, that's a little scary.

So Charlie just drifted away. He came to rehearsal late, he left early, he wasn't really there when he was rehearsing—that kind of stuff.

As Charlie absented himself more and more, I started filling in. At first I would just play with the guys to warm them up. Then gradually I began to play with the band as they rehearsed their set. Teddy and I wrote two new songs together: "Mary, Quite Contrary" and "River Kisses."

Always, I got right out of the way when Charlie showed up. But it reached a point fairly quickly (by then we rehearsed *four* nights a week) where they didn't get much done when Charlie showed up because he and Teddy would spend all their time at each other's throats because Charlie didn't know the new songs, he'd forgotten his bass lines on the other stuff, and he just didn't play with any emotion anymore. But he really dug listening to us. It seemed he loved the music, but he didn't love *playing* the music. And he and Teddy couldn't/wouldn't resolve what that meant, so they fought instead. Then came the time when Charlie stopped showing up at all. We just went ahead. We even played three shows in December.

I didn't know how to feel about it, Angel.

I don't know how to feel now.

In a way, I think it must be like a second marriage.

You either know they love you as you or you

wonder.

At some point, though, you have to stop wondering.

I stopped wondering—you should, too.

Then, just before exams, at our last rehearsal in Chapel Hill before the holidays, Charlie walked in as we were doing our last three numbers. He didn't say anything, and to this day I don't think anyone noticed him but me. Maybe it was because I was and am so sensitive about what he gave me by giving me the band. By this time, mid-December, Teddy and the rest of us had even talked about a name change. I'd tossed out The Lost Generation one night after rehearsal when I'd had a few beers. Everyone had liked it; Mick and Sid were all set to rename the band. But Teddy seemed to be waiting for something; that night when Charlie showed up, he got it.

When we finished playing, Teddy looked over at Charlie. "So. What'd you think?" he asked.

Charlie just nodded his head in that way he does that says, *I'm way ahead of you.* Then he said out loud, "This band can go all the way. Don't you think so, Jay?"

I was standing there with my head down, feeling guilty, and I didn't realize for a second that he'd addressed his question to me. Then I noticed that they were all looking at me instead of at Teddy.

I turned to Charlie. He had that homespun look of wisdom he usually gets on his face when he knows he's got you. Then, I looked at Teddy again. He had that *Go ahead* expression he's so famous for.

I didn't look at Mick or Sid. I guess I didn't feel they were involved, even though they were right there, and integral members of the band. It just seemed like it was about Charlie, Teddy, and me.

I nodded *yes* in answer to Charlie.

I saw this sad little light pass across Charlie's eyes as he smiled at me.

Teddy looked surprised; I guess I mention it because he so rarely does.

Then Charlie asked quietly, "What are you going to call it?" He meant the band.

"The Lost Generation." Only after he'd answered did Teddy look at Charlie.

"Cool name." Charlie smiled.

Then Teddy smiled. "Jay thought of it," he said.

And they both smiled at me. And I smiled.

Then we all went out and had a bunch of beers to celebrate.

Neither Teddy nor Charlie ever spoke to me about it again.

Maybe they talked it over between themselves, but I never felt they did. That's the thing at work between them that I was talking about earlier, I guess. They just knew it would be okay for it to be this way.

So Nothing Sacred ended and The Lost Generation began.

You know what I mean by all this.
You know what I'm trying to tell you.
That's how things happen, Angel.
That's how things happen.
Things end—things begin again.

Love,
Jay

JAY'S BOOK OF DAYS

The night before we played the show in Baton Rouge, I stood on a pier and watched fog swallow an entire bridge across the Mississippi. I called out to you, but perhaps not loudly enough because you did not come to me.

Loneliness as a reward . . .

Smiling is a skill I have not developed very well.

Life as change . . . Yeah, well . . .

My son's eyes as he looked at a crawfish . . .

Some people haven't had all the advantages I've had. (Fitzgerald)

Their parents send them off to school. . . . But there it's "everyone is the same. . . ."
(Hatter/Breeze, from "Boys With Guitars and Dreams")

A telephone call can make all the difference.

Faith like a dog. Fidelity.

I cannot paint what then I was.
(Wordsworth)

If music be the food of love, what then be the food of music?

How many juxtapositions are not incongruous?

Beware of people who begin conversations with, "I used to be in a band. . . ."

Pickles . . . I don't know why. . . .

You can smell the rain and you can hear the wind— how cool is that?

Carolina Blues

December 21, 1991
Chapal Hill

Dearnesst Angel,

Why, why, why, why, why, hwy, why, hwy, why, why, hwy, hwy, hwy, why, why, why, why, hwy, hwy, why, why, why, whhy. why, hwy, why, why, why, why?

Baby, oh, baby, ohbaby, obaaby, aobaaaby . . . . . .
. . . .
I.m sorry. Shouldn't wrte.. I'mtodrukn, I think its 2anm......... How diod i get all thos dost?

Got hedphones on, listeing to Robet Plant. Led Zep bigger than us. Biger than everyboy.

Biig Sadnees. Too drun..... What's with goddam dots?

Love you forever.. Ghey wow....
always dots.

December 22, 1991
2:18 P.M.

Dear Angel,

I tried to write after I got home last night. You see the result. Drank a pint of brandy. Didn't seem enough, so I went to work on another. Wrote the stuff above somewhere around the end of the first bottle. Fell off my swivel chair shortly after that (I think). Spilled most of the second bottle on the carpet. Woke up breathing alcohol fumes. Broke another pair of headphones. When I fell, I ripped the male jack out of the female jack.

Male jack. Female jack. God, I'm pathetic.

You know, the sound of these computer keys is like hammers on my skull. Hangover from hell. Going to town and getting new headphones. Back in a bit.

Took me a while, I guess. I went by to see Charlie Beagle. We ended up going out for dinner. Autographs? Sure. Signed four. Had a couple of drinks, too. Boy, howdy, I feel better.

Bought three new sets of headphones. At least I won't have to go to the store for new ones for a couple of months, maybe.

I know I'm avoiding the issue of this letter, but I just don't want to talk about it right now. Shit, Angel, it doesn't seem like you're gone yet.

Marlene called from Munich. Jakob was ecstatic about his computer. Good suggestion. He turned fifteen on the 12th, the day after you turned twenty-four. Somebody told me (or I read somewhere) that Brian Jones left maybe ten illegitimate children. Who's Brian Jones? Dammit, Angel, you're such a baby. Brian was an original member of The Rolling Stones. Died in July of 1969, a month after he was

41

kicked out of the band.

If I die tomorrow, I leave only one (I think). Guess that makes me nine illegitimate children more responsible than Brian Jones.

I'm so proud of myself.

Marlene was the first to tell me I've got *Weltschmerz*. World Sorrow. Melancholy. The Big Sadness.

Am I blue? (That's the title of an old Billie Holiday song, isn't it?)

By now I should be used to people being unable to accept things about me, but I guess I'm not. You have to understand, Angel. Money and fame and all that have opened a lot of doors for me. People never tell me no (well, almost never).

I can't help but think, in spite of all you say, that my going on tour again is why you've left me.

You've left me.

I'm going to go buy some more brandy.

December 23, 1991
1:25 A.M.

Dear, dear Angel,

I'm having a blue Christmas. Have to leave in the afternoon for my parents' house. They still live in Reidsville. You know that. Sometimes they go to the cottage I bought for them on Jekyll Island, but this year they're staying home. So Marshall and I can "come home" for Christmas.

Home. Almost my entire adult life has been lived in hotel rooms, resort condos, and rented mansions. It's been luxurious, but it hasn't been home.

This house I'm sitting in while writing to you is the first "home" I've ever owned (that I actually lived in). I'd lived in it a year before I met you.

You made it a home.

Angel, what will I do without you?

Drunl;   I kow what yu say.

   For am in th e mornig.

GODADMITT   IT, Angle   you   legt   me. Crikstmas.   I love you.

   Love you, love uyo loveyou,,,   are these dots agin?   Can't see.../,'l   I",m goimg to bde.

               Love,   Jay

December 23, 1991
3:14 P.M.

My Angel,

The house is absolutely still. I have the headphones hanging around my neck.

I've been listening to playbacks of the material for a new album. I know. You think going back into the music will kill me.

So what?

You won't be there to see it, will you?

The house is absolutely still. It's two days before Christmas.

We're thinking of two possible titles for the new album: *April is the Cruelest Month* from "The Wasteland" by Eliot, or *Lovely, Dark, and Deep* from Frost's "Stopping by Woods on a Snowy Evening."

I don't know why I'm telling you this. You don't want to know. You don't care. You're like everyone else, I guess. It's always, "Oh, wow, there he is. Jay Breeze. The Rock Star. Will he give me his autograph? Will he talk with me? Will he play and sing for me? Will he give me some of his money? Will he sleep with me?"

Never, Angel. You're not like them. You're not like anyone else. You would never ask for anything. You'd rather die.

Don't think I don't understand.

That's what scares me.

You understand.

Perfectly.

I don't know how.

The truth is you're not like anyone else. Why? Why do you get me when no one else does? Why do I get you when I don't get anyone else? No walls. Ever.

Got to get going. Talk to you tonight.

Love,

Jay

Oh, Angel,

Came in about an hour ago. Marshall and I were out at a round of Christmas parties. I've had a few drinks but none of the unholy stuff I've been drinking the last couple of days.

Marsh has been great. You know how funny he is. Grandmother (Mom's mom) always said he got the personality and I got the looks. Yeah. Right.

Anyway, we made the rounds. The people who grew up with me made a big issue out of knowing me. People who never knew me but had (of course?) heard of me treated me as if I were—what? The two-headed calf at the circus? No, that's not it. What's it like, Angel?

This is where you would have exactly the right description for how things were. You would have sized everything up and given me some very sensible observation about the behavior of all these people. Then I would write it down here as I've written down so many of the things you've said to me.

But you've left me.

The house is absolutely still.

What did you promise your mother, Angel?

Did you promise to kill me?

You're going to, you know.

I'm going to see if Marsh has a bottle.

If he doesn't, I'll get one from the car.

I'm weak and I'm bad, Angel.

You're right not to love me.

Nobody should.

`It id 5'37 A>M.   Gon agan.   Noyu
      no god..   NO GOOD.
  SHIt.   Tuned on caaspitol letters.
        Sorry. Always so soory.
    Go bed now.   Mars helping me. By
Angel. Love always.

December 24, 1991
12:18 P.M.

Well, Angel,

I'm sitting here with the hangover from hell at
my Aunt Barbara's house. She has been quietly and
reprovingly giving me tomato juice with shots of
Worcestershire sauce. I keep asking for vodka, too,
but she won't give.

Merry Christmas, Angel.

Tell you a story. When I was eleven or twelve, I
used to mow my Aunt Barbara's lawn every week.
While I mowed I listened to a transistor radio. It was
red and had a white cord with a single earplug. The
cord was just long enough to reach from the radio in
my shorts pocket to my right ear.

I would mow and sing at the top of my lungs
along with the British Invasion groups: The Beatles,
of course; The Rolling Stones; The Animals; The
Kinks. I had the best time, you know?

This drove my Aunt Barbara crazy. She would
call me up to her screened back porch and give me a
glass of lemonade or iced tea or milk and maybe a

sandwich or a piece of fruit pie. Then she would fetch a volume of *The Harvard Classics* and have me read to her to prove that rock-and-roll wasn't rotting my brain. That summer I got through Machiavelli's *The Prince* and Thomas More's *Utopia*. And I learned the words to "Satisfaction" by The Stones and The Beatles' "Help."

And it all made sense. I began to think of The Rolling Stones as Machiavellian and of The Beatles as Utopian (probably because I thought Utopia was supposed to be a nice place and The Beatles seemed nicer than The Stones). Maybe that's what's meant by a liberal education.

You know, Angel, I told Ringo this story at a party in L.A. We sat on one of those sectional sofas that was about a half-mile long and stretched along the walls of this room that had floor-to-ceiling windows looking out over Malibu Canyon. He just sat quietly and listened. When I finished he said, "Imagine. A kid in a little town in North Carolina listening to us on a transistor. And now you're here. Imagine." Then he got up and went to pee or something.

I have no idea what the hell it means, Angel.

So what's new, right?

Aunt Barbara wants to know what I'm writing. I've told her a letter. I guess that's what this is. I'm writing you a letter, Angel. I'll probably write you a million letters. You're the person I tell everything to, Angel.

What will I do with you gone?

If I wrote a million letters, would you read them?

You would.

I love you so much. You gotta come back.

December 24, 1991
11:48 P.M.

Goddammit, Angel,

We just got off the phone. The thing that costs me the most is your ability to push me away. Your coldness (whether it was conscious or unconscious I can't say) hurt me worse than anything you could ever do to me. I feel a knife in my heart—it has your name on it. (I know—sounds like one of our song lyrics.)

I realize now I will never send you this letter. I will never send you any of the million letters I will probably write. But because I can't keep anything from you, I won't be able not to. You know what is in my heart and soul anyway.

What I will try to tell you is what I think is happening.

What is happening, Angel?

Am I being punished by God because I play evil rock-and-roll? Is the person I have loved most in my life to be taken from me because of this?

I don't believe it.

I'm too caught up in my own myth.

There's a song by Argent called "God Gave Rock and Roll to You." I think that's true.

Rock's like religion, Angel. I mean, concerts are like church, aren't they? Like religious rituals, anyway. All that holding lights to the sky and stuff. On stage is where I feel closest to God, Angel. I feel sanctified. Holy. The music, the crowd, the lights—it all reaches my soul.

I think you may come back to me.

It feels right now as if you will.

Just checked my watch. It's Christmas.

There are so few things that bring joy, Angel. So few things that touch the soul. The music does that for me.

Christmas does it. You do it.

To be able to say that—that someone gives me joy—scares me, Angel. To say that you touch my soul seems too small. You complete my soul. I complete yours. We have completeness of the soul.

Yeah, I'm too devoted. To you, to the music, to—Christmas?

I don't really know what else.

I feel I can do anything if you're there, Angel.

What a gift.

It's Christmas.

The house is absolutely still.

You never leave me—you know?

That's the gift, isn't it? Someone who is always there. For each person, someone who is always there.

You are always there for me, Angel.

Thank you.

Merry Christmas.

Oh! There's the phone.

God bless us every one. . . .

Love,
Jay

JAY'S BOOK OF DAYS

Night is somehow better than day.

Once I stood on a hill in eastern Colorado and watched a tornado move through a western Kansas village several miles away. I wanted very much to go and stand in the tornado's path. Just to see. I wonder how many other people feel this way?

You are always with me, a fleeting presence at the edge of my peripheral vision, whispering to me at a volume too soft for me to make out the words. But I would know the voice anywhere.

Sometimes life is fucking boring.

I left her because I got tired of having to lie when she asked me, "What are you thinking?"

If you hadn't spoken first . . . I don't know. I think I would have, but I don't know. . . . It scares me to think about it.

Such, such is life.
(Edward Lear)

Rock music is the twentieth century art form.

Something like 96% of rock songs are about love.

Yes. (Can you think of a better word?)

Fame is the twentieth century art form.

All I ever did was go to school; then I became a millionaire rock star. What do I know?

Everybody . . . everywhere . . . every time . . .

I think people who play the clarinet must feel lonelier than the rest of us.

I like to drive fast on snowy roads . . . what this says about me . . .

The past is what the future thought it was.

Blondes and redheads . . . brunettes are too much trouble. . . .

The Balcony Scene

Dear Angel,

I am starting to come to some sense of myself now. The first thing I have done since beginning to sober up is get my laptop and start writing to you. This may prove once and for all that I am crazy.

This is all I can think to do, Angel. Somehow I know that if I talk to you everything will be all right. But how can I talk to you?

You're dead, Angel.

This is the first time I've said it. This is the first time I've let myself believe it.

What will I do?

Angel, I must say some things. I'm not sure how coherent I can be—or how coherent I am or ever will be again.

It feels as if someone has taken a shotgun and blown a gaping hole through my life.

What in the hell were you thinking, Angel?

Drunk driving. What have I told you?

I know. I do it. All the time. I should be the one dead.

I've explained this to you. I've lived two or three lifetimes in these seventeen years I've been a (God forgive me) rock star. My life is charmed.

No, this does not justify my self-destructiveness. My being so wrong will not make you right, then, will it?

Or alive . . .

You are the only woman who ever made me believe that she truly loved me.

I have always felt pretty much alone in the midst of it all, you know? As if I was standing in the center of a tornado that whirled around me and moved as I moved, never touching me, always moving about me. Always letting me alone. Leaving me alone. Left alone . . . (I'm lyricising again. . . .)

I feel the most alone right now that I have ever felt in my life.

Oh, Angel, I love you so. Truly. With all my heart and soul. Always. Forever.

And now it's too late to tell you again. One last time.

I know. I told you plenty.

I'd like to tell you a story—a story that would finally make you see that although saner people might love you better, no one could love you more.

Are you as alone as I am?

Okay, okay. Here's the story.

If you look up "decadence" in the dictionary, you'll probably find a picture of New Orleans. It's a great town to go wrong in. I know. I've gone wrong there several times.

Had a lot of fun.

I think.

There are so many balconies in New Orleans.

You walk through the French Quarter and all you see are these beautiful balconies. Some are tilted toward the street because the houses have shifted or settled or something. They look as if they'd be easy to fall from. Even easier to jump from.

The beer you drink in New Orleans is Dixie.

There's a place called Pat O'Brien's. They serve a drink called a Hurricane. God only knows what's in it.

I started out from the Chateau de Roi Marque. Nice hotel. Teddy and Mick were chatting up some girls in the bar. I watched for a while and had a few Dixies. Got the start of a buzz, then made my way outside. Only had to sign two autographs. One nice thing about really expensive hotels is that people who stay in them like to think they're too cool to ask a rock star for his autograph. Or they're too old to give a damn. Either way . . . you know?

Wandered down to Bourbon Street. Ran into Sid who'd gone out earlier. We hadn't talked thirty seconds when college kids surrounded us. We signed some autographs, then flagged a taxi. Sid got out after two blocks. I got the driver to circle back to Bourbon.

Met Sid again at this dive called Johnny White's. We always eat there when we're in New Orleans. Even though it was January, it was in the sixties (at night, no less), so we sat out on the balcony. "Bastard lists like the deck of the Titanic," Sid said. So we sang a stanza of "Nearer, My God, to Thee."

Some asshole at the next table told us to shut up, then slobbered all over us when his friends told him who we were.

Drank a few more Dixies. Sid drank those damned Blackened Voodoos.

Sid ate blackened snapper. I had cuisses de grenouilles. Frog legs. Say it with me—*kwees duh grin oo yuh*. I'm a gourmand—or a fool. Maybe both.

You know, I just thought about the first time I saw you across the room in that class we took together when I'd come back to UNC last year to finish my BA, after I'd "retired"—so to speak. I thought you were the most beautiful woman I'd ever seen in my life.

I still think that.

I will always think that.

I wonder what people will think if they read this. They may not like my little digressions, my little rhapsodies. If they don't, fuck them. They won't get it anyway. They never could.

This is assuming that people get to read this stuff. Knowing me, I'll destroy it all when I find out I'm dying (of something God-awful for sure) and no one will ever get to understand why an aging (thirty-eight!) rock star and a twenty-two-year-old psychologist-to-be fell in love against the wishes of families, friends, and much of Western civilization.

Some things are just going to be, you know? Maybe it's proof of God's existence. That's how I like to think of it.

Yeah, I'm off the subject.

Okay. The story.

We sat on the balcony at Johnny White's and got pretty toasted. The asshole at the next table kept buying us beers to apologize. Foolish on his part . . . rock stars drink a lot.

Finally, Jacques, our waiter, whispered that he needed to close down. When we got up from the table, Sid staggered over to the railing to look at the design (you know how all those New Orleans wrought-iron balconies have such elaborate designs) and almost fell over. Jacques and one of the guys from the next table grabbed him.

I went over to the railing.

It was probably fifteen or twenty feet down to the

street. After all those beers I felt like I might go over myself. I leaned out into the New Orleans night with all its filth and sound and grasping, and whispered, "Romeo, Romeo!/ Wherefore art thou Romeo?"

I *was* Romeo for a while. Early on it was, "Wow, all these girls. And I can have any of them. All of them."

But I found I couldn't do that. Couldn't do that at all. I have to feel something. And I can't fake it. And there's no feeling to that stuff . . . well, you know, emotion. . . .

In a way it was much easier for me before you. It was easy when everyone wanted me and I didn't want anyone. When people loved me and I could love them back in this Jesus-like way. Even the women (more or less, mostly less) I got involved with I felt I was doing a kindness to.

(Yeah, this is just about the height of arrogance. I don't mean it to be. It was protection. Jay the Big Star, you know? Not me.)

Of all the things about you, I think I love the way you walk the most. It's a real woman's walk. You sort of roll side to side the way a good sailboat does in a strong wind, when the waves are making whitecaps.

I love sailing. I love a good sailboat. I love you. Loving you is like sailing. Good sailing when you're excited and scared at the same time, flying almost and not caring if you ever stop or come back. Makes your heart stop.

You always make mine stop.

There was nothing else to prove. Nothing to test. Sometimes, to test might be the wrong thing. Sometimes we must trust and love and risk—but not ruin—ourselves.

I mean, really. Drunk driving. After we talked about how sensible and responsible we needed to be. For each other. Just in case. Because we always knew we'd find each other again. Even if we went apart for awhile.

Well, we did go apart.

You left me.

Then you died.

Will we find each other again? Sometimes I think yes, sometimes no.

All I know is I miss you.

January 31, 1992
2:31 P.M.

Dear Angel,

Well, it's been a couple of days. Life on the road, you know? Played concerts in Houston and Dallas. Good shows, actually.

Some *alternative*-music asshole (What kind of term is that, anyway? Alternative. Jesus. Give me a break. We all play rock.) was complaining about all the *dinosaur* rockers out on tour. He mentioned us specifically.

Well, fuck him. At least we can play. There weren't ten thousand little half-assed recording studios and record companies around for us. We had to be able to play *before* we made records. All these little snot-nosed, paisley-wearing, tie-dyed hippie wannabes and nose-pierced, spike-haired faux-punks can kiss my ass.

Ooh, Jay's mad, she says.

And then you laugh.

That raucous laugh that makes me see I'm as silly as they are.

That laugh.

I'll never hear it again.

And I'll never stop hearing it.

Maybe it was your laugh that made me love you.

I know. The story. Where was I?

Oh, yeah. Well, these two guys are holding Sid up from the railing and I'm standing there thinking about jumping. You know, stuff like whether a fall of twenty feet would be enough to kill me. So I could be with you. Or if it would just maim me badly so I'd end up in a hospital bed unable to do anything but lie there and think about you for years and years.

I say that as if it were somehow different from what I do now. I was thinking about how once, last fall I guess it was, you'd been at some frat party with an old flame. Anyway, you'd had a few so you decided to ditch the poor sod and come out to my house. I was sitting in the den with my headphones on, so you were able to let yourself in without my hearing you. And you came right in and sat on my lap. And you kissed me. And when I get to heaven and God asks me what was the happiest moment of my life, that's the one I'll mention.

We were never your average couple. Average couples can't love each other the way we do. "Dull sublunary lovers" we weren't.

It's a quote from a John Donne poem, Angel. A poem called, "A Valediction: Forbidding Mourning."

I won't mourn, Angel. I will still love you. And

eventually I'll be with you.

I have to get ready for the show. I'll finish the story about New Orleans later. I know, I know. I don't mean to make you crazy doing that.

February 1, 1992
2:15 A.M.

Dear Angel,

I've been off the stage for a couple of hours now. I've had a shower, some food, and a few drinks. Maybe it's me, but the UTEP audience just wasn't into the show. I kept getting the vibe that East Coast college boys playing Beatles-influenced songs about WASP relationships didn't seem to strike a chord with them.

Well, as Teddy said at one of our first gigs, we've got their money.

Now we have a few days off. Teddy and I are going skiing in New Mexico. Taos or maybe Angel Fire. Probably Angel Fire. Taos is full of people like us. You know—famous people. Or worse, people who get excited about being around famous people.

All right. Finally. Here's what happened in New Orleans.

So the guys pull Sid back from the railing. Then everybody is so relieved that he didn't get killed that the management pays our bill. I insist that they pay the bill for the folks at the next table, too, since they helped save Sid's life. When I ask them to pay the bill of everyone who comes in during Mardi Gras, they laugh and throw us out.

Sid and I stand around for a little while in front of Johnny White's, while groups of people go by and point at us and whisper to each other. Sid yells at one group of baby boomer couples, "Hey, is my fly open or something? Or are you so backward you've never seen a rock star before?"

They laugh. As if he'd told them a joke.

See what I mean about people not getting it, Angel? These stupid people think we're going to be like The Beatles in *A Hard Day's Night*. Cute, lovable chaps with just a funny flicker of attitude. They think they're in on the joke.

Remember how you hated it when we'd be out to dinner and people would worry the hell out of me for autographs so that half the time I wouldn't eat?

I hated it, too. Only I couldn't say so because if I did I'd just lose it and become a complete asshole and scream at everybody who came close. Or tried to.

Can't live like that, Angel. I mean, I accepted certain turf when I accepted money and fame.

Something's wrong somewhere, sweetheart.

I should not have to be a target for people's wishes, dreams, and fantasies. Yeah, maybe I'm an artist. Maybe I've spoken to a lot of people through music. Maybe I've articulated some of their feelings about love or loss or life. But really, it's the music that's done that.

It's art that's done that.

And I'm the artist. I'm not the art.

I guess that's why I'm always uncomfortable when some man wants to buy me meals or drinks or when some woman comes on to me because I'm Jay Breeze.

It's not me they want to thank. It's the music. It's the art.

This is all getting too complicated. I'm going to sleep.

Hi, Angel,

Hey. I just got up a little while ago, when Paul came by to bang on the door to make sure I was still alive. I always answer the wake-up phone calls they give, then go back to sleep (as everyone does), so part of Paul's job is to try to get us awake so we can go wherever it is we're supposed to go and do whatever it is we're supposed to do.

Yeah, I'm pretty spoiled, all right.

Oh. I still need to tell you what happened in New Orleans. Okay, okay. I know it's about time.

You know, it's important to be in touch with you.

A lot of the time I feel like you hear what I think.

Cool.

Sid and I were pretty buzzed when we left Johnny White's. The sensible thing to do would have been to go back to the hotel. Or at least call someone in our entourage so they could come and get us.

We didn't do either, of course.

What we did was wind up in the hands of about five or six college girls. They were LSU students out

61

for a bit of fun in The Big Easy. Two of them had been to the show the night before. They were all pretty excited to be out on the town with a couple of "real live" rock stars.

Yeah, they were all sort of pretty in that college-girl way. Youth and freshness and all that.

No, I didn't fall in love with any of them. It wasn't like that. It was just fun. They were kids and they thought we were so great and it was enjoyable to let them think that for the evening.

Anyway, that's how we ended up at Pat O'Brien's. One of the girls said it was great, so we went there.

Actually, it was pretty nice. There are two or three bars. We went in them all. Sid and I tried to pay for everyone's drinks all the time, but the girls wouldn't hear of it. They each bought a round.

Sid and I were drinking these things called Hurricanes. I'm damned if I know what's in them. Pure intoxicant, evidently.

We were pretty shit-faced when the police took us back to our hotel.

The police. Why the police?

Well may you ask, love of my life.

It was my fault.

After a few of these Hurricane drinks, I took it into my head to go exploring. When you enter Pat O'Brien's, you walk in through a kind of entranceway with a bar on either side. Then you come out into this big, beautiful courtyard that's surrounded by buildings three or four stories high.

And there are all these balconies.

Actually, the way they're all together, they're more like those walkways at Holiday Inns.

No, that's not fair. They're much nicer than that.

They play a part in this. Which is why I'm going on so about them.

Somehow I got myself up to a balcony three stories above the courtyard. I don't know how I got there. I remember thinking I wanted to be up there and then I was.

So I was standing on the balcony, leaning on the lovely wrought-iron railing and looking down at Sid sitting at a lovely wrought-iron table in a lovely wrought-iron chair and talking to the lovely not-wrought-iron coeds. And there were other people there, too. All sitting in lovely wrought-iron chairs at lovely wrought-iron tables and having lovely drinks with other lovely people.

It *was* all lovely, Angel. Too lovely for me. And too far away.

So I climbed up on the railing. And I stood with my arms around a post and watched everyone. And then a woman looked up and saw me.

And she yelled.

She yelled, "My God, he's going to jump!"

Until that moment I hadn't thought of jumping, Angel. I just got up on the railing to look at everybody in a different way. But then she yelled. That woman yelled. And I thought (maybe it was the booze) that I *should* jump. I really hate to let people down.

And then I thought, because I was way high, I guess (both in the air and from the drinking), that jumping would be a way. A way back to you. That it would only hurt a second when I hit the courtyard, and then I'd see you again. And you would take me into your arms and it wouldn't hurt anymore. Ever.

Boy, that was tempting, Angel.

63

But then Sid saved me.

He saw me up there on the railing after the woman yelled. I must have been swaying some (I was drunk, after all). So he got up from his chair and meandered over to a spot directly below me. (He was smashed, too.) "Jay, yo, Jay," he hollered up at me.

"Yeah?"

He took a step back, involuntarily. "Whatcha doin'?"

"Just standing here, looking down at everybody." I leaned against the post and my foot slipped a little. I heard gasps, which I thought at the time were angel voices, but I know now were just gasps.

"You thinking about jumping?" Sid hollered.

"Not before, but just now I was," I hollered back.

"On account of Angel?" (He said your real name, but I promised never to write it here, so I've put in Angel.)

"Yeah." I clutched the pole tighter, because I knew then that I didn't want to die. I didn't know if I wanted to live, but I didn't want to die.

"But what about Houston?" Sid yelled.

"Houston?" I yelled back.

"We have to play there tomorrow night." He held out his hands in the familiar *Search me* gesture.

"Yeah? So?"

"Jay, if you jump, we'll have to cancel. You know how Teddy gets if we think we have to cancel." Then he grinned.

Sid has a great grin, Angel. Even from a long way away, a long way up, it's a great grin. "What should I do?" I asked, just messing around.

"Come on down and let's have another drink with these pretty girls," Sid yelled. Then he grinned again.

64

"Okay." And I got off the railing. Just as I was back down on the balcony, several firemen (and some cops) came rushing into the courtyard. Very strange. They told me to stay where I was, which was fine with me because I couldn't have figured out how to get back down to the courtyard I don't think. Then, the firemen came and got me and took me down to the courtyard, and the cops talked to me and Sid for a long time and we convinced them that we were only clowning around, drunk and all like that, and then we were going to have another drink with the college girls but the cops had sent them away, and then the cops insisted on taking us back to the hotel and Paul and Van and Teddy and Mick and everyone met us in the lobby and we talked to them and I got yelled at for being foolish but not for the other thing, the part about you that I talked with Sid about and he never told anyone, and I appreciated that and told him so later in Dallas.

And then we went to Houston.

That's what happened in New Orleans.

Got to go. Teddy and I are flying up to Taos.

Talk to you later

Love,
Jay

JAY'S BOOK OF DAYS

I realized that trouble, real trouble, was something to be avoided, inasmuch as once it passed by, you have only yourself to answer to, even if, as I was, you are the cause of nothing.
(Richard Ford)

I have spread my dreams under your feet;
Tread softly, because you tread on my dreams.
(Yeats)

The rain is something I understand.

No one, I think, is in my tree.
(John Lennon)

I would never have thought sadness to have blue eyes.

People don't read enough poetry.

Accepting a love as inevitable.

Play the guitar.

I would like to say that I am a man more sinned against than sinning, but I'm not sure how that will hold up in the court where I am apt to be tried.

When I am not with you and you think of me, it is because I am missing you.

Other than love, what really matters?

You can scream at IHOP if you like, but they do call the police. . . .

It takes much longer to be simple than it does to be complicated.

I don't care if I'm right—I'm trying to have a good time. . . .

Received Wisdom

February 5, 1992
11:30 P.M.

Dear Angel,

The Albuquerque show was a mess. It started snowing the morning of the show and the trucks carrying our equipment couldn't get into town. Paul, Scott, and Van spent the entire day desperately phoning every music store and sound professional in Albuquerque and Santa Fe—just in case—trying to round up the right equipment so that we could do the concert. The weather got progressively worse as the day wore on.

Teddy and I had flown up to Taos to ski three days before; we quit at lunchtime and started for Albuquerque, but we could only get as far as Santa Fe in a rented Jeep and that took us about four hours. They were going to send a snowplow kind of vehicle or something for us, but someone with better sense than us nixed that. Besides, with the weather so bad, there wasn't going to be a show that night anyway. So Teddy and I wound up checked into a hotel called the Inn of the Governors.

We tried to check into a place called the El Dorado, but it's part of the Quality Inn corporation and we're banned from those places for life. When Teddy gave them his AE card to pay for the room, some ID system on their computer spit out our names as belonging to bad, bad boys. The manager, a guy about thirty-five who thought he was cool, came to the desk and told us politely that we couldn't stay with them but that he'd be delighted to find us comparable accommodations.

The El Dorado's lobby was really busy, so it didn't take Teddy long to gather a crowd once he started raising hell at the desk clerks and the manager. He just bashed the poor guy about sending us out into a howling blizzard because of prejudice against poor, underprivileged rock stars like us. I stood by and smiled at the crowd. People like me when I smile. I guess because I don't very often.

I should explain why we're banned with a "for example." During the 1978 tour of the Southwest—for example—we trashed two rooms of the Quality Inn South in Dallas. It started innocently enough. Mick and I had a room adjoining Teddy and Sid's. We couldn't get the connecting door to unlock, even though hotel management assured us it would open. We had a big party going (surprise) and were all pretty drunk when the guy arrived to get the door open for us. When he couldn't unlock it, for some reason we all got pissed off. We threw some furniture at the door and Paul and Van, pretty big guys, tried bashing the door down. Even that didn't work.

Finally Mick got a fire axe (from where I have no idea) and we chopped through the door, all the time laughing and yelling, "No fire! No fire!" Sid and I got into the spirit and pulled the pieces of the door off its hinges and threw them off our balcony and onto the deck by the swimming pool. Teddy got some charcoal lighter fluid from somewhere.

The next thing I remember is cops and fire trucks arriving and we're down by the pool dancing naked with some girls (yeah, they're naked, too), and then we all get led away with sheets wrapped around us. That cost us some money and evidently raised questions in the minds of the Quality Inn corporation's management about the wisdom of allowing us as guests in their hotels.

Now do you understand? Yes, Angel, we've been bad boys. Quite often, actually.

Meanwhile, the hotel manager lost his cool and announced to the lobby at large, "You see, Mr. Hatter, corporate records show that you and your friend Mr. Breeze are responsible, in concert with a Mr. (he checked a computer screen) Mick Norris and a Mr. Sid (screen again) Vegas for seriously damaging some (screen again) *fourteen* rooms in Quality Inns scattered across the country from Boston to Dallas."

I need to mention something here, Angel. This asshole knew who we were. Everybody his age and with his socio-economic background knows who we are. I bet he had two or three of our albums. I mean this guy was no country music or R & B fan. You could smell his Ralph Lauren Polo. He listened to us in college. Probably still listened to us. I could see him cranking up "Mary, Quite Contrary" in the car when we came on the radio as he drove home listening to his favorite classic rock station. I couldn't figure out why he wanted to make a production of throwing us out of his hotel.

Then I noticed the girl. She must've been about twenty. His favorite night clerk, I was betting. Dark hair and eyes. Very pretty. Watching first him, then us. He could smell her indecision about who was more attractive, so he had to do something. He was playing the big man for her. Showing her that even famous rock stars couldn't fuck with him.

70

Teddy looked at me. "Is that right?"

I shrugged. "I thought it was closer to twenty. How about Denver? And San Diego? And Atlanta? And . . ."

Teddy shook his head. "No, those were Holiday Inns."

People had been gathering as we wrangled with the hotel manager, and there had been two different waves of murmuring, building like swells off the North Shore. One wave was the "Is it really them?" wave. The other was the "They're not going to give them a room? In this blizzard? Don't they know who these guys are?" wave.

Then it was suddenly quiet.

It was that weird quiet that sometimes comes over a crowd for maybe twenty seconds before the band comes on stage. It was that quiet that you know is going to explode into pandemonium. That hotel manager hadn't grasped what was about to happen to him. That lobby full of thirty-somethings coming from or going to Taos was going to leap on him like a pack of coyotes on a lost lamb.

One of the anomalies of the rock star profession, Angel (I guess one can call it a profession), is that no matter what kinds of assholes we are, our fans will defend us tooth and nail.

About then the manager realized what deep shit he was in. He went pale and took a half step back from the desk as if readying himself to run.

I figured somebody better do something.

I leaned over the desk and motioned to the manager. He hesitated. I motioned again, this time more urgently. For some reason, as I did so I thought of the little tramp in Chaplin's *The Gold Rush* motioning impatiently to his prospector pal to pull him out of the cabin that's about to go over a cliff. He stepped over and leaned close.

"Look," I said quietly, matter-of-factly, "give us somewhere to go right now, then come back here and find us a room in a hotel close by. Then see to it that we get there as quickly and comfortably as possible."

The manager looked out across the crowd that was just starting to reach that Banzai Pipeline crest. He drew himself up and said, "Mr. Hatter, Mr. Breeze, on behalf of the Quality Inn corporation, we'd like to offer you a comfortable place to relax while we arrange for your alternate accommodations. I suggest—"

The cute desk clerk, who'd sort of just stood there wide-eyed while Teddy and the manager wrangled, had gotten busy. She handed her boss a telephone receiver. "This is the Inn of the Governors, sir," she whispered. "They've got a suite ready for these gentlemen, and they're sending someone in a Jeep to pick them up. They'll be here in thirty minutes."

Manager-Boy took the receiver and spoke briefly. "Everything is arranged," he said theatrically. "Now if you'll follow me—" He came from behind the desk and picked up my bag. Teddy stopped him.

"Acknowledge the girl for what she did," he said quietly.

"What do you mean?" asked the manager.

"She saved your ass," I said, taking my bag away from him. "Tell this crowd she did."

His expression told me he wasn't going to last much longer in the hospitality industry if more clients like us came along.

"Thank you, Brooke, for arranging for Mr.

Hatter's and Mr. Breeze's accommodations." He smiled as if someone had just stuck a branding iron against his ass. He took my bag, picked up Teddy's, and started for the bar.

"Yes, Brooke, thank you. Look, we're going to be at the Inn of the Governors. When you finish your shift, come on over and we'll hang out. I'll tell you about some of the interesting things that have happened to me in hotels," Teddy said, loudly enough for everybody in the lobby to hear.

I just smiled at her and winked.

Yeah, Angel, she came over. She hooked up with Teddy.

We followed The Pompous One toward the bar. The crowd parted for us like the Red Sea. Some of the weird stuff that always used to happen when we walked through a crowd happened. A woman stepped out of the crowd and kissed Teddy on the cheek, then ducked back into the mob. She must've been about forty. As I passed her I noticed a guy looking at her— must've been her husband—like she'd just broken his heart. Another woman stepped out and touched my hair, just drew the back of her hand across it as I passed. I glanced back and she was holding her hand and looking at it as if she'd burned it or gotten something on it. Guys were saying stuff to us like, "Hey, Teddy," or, "Cool hair, Jay." It was such an old-fashioned moment.

The kids just don't react that way now. They talk to you like you're anybody else. That damned Cobain and Michael Stipe are ruining it for everybody.

It was after five by then and Teddy went

immediately to the phone in the bar and called Albuquerque to tell them where we would be. The show was definitely cancelled. We heard the announcement on a radio playing in the bar. I ordered us a couple of beers and told the bartender to charge them to Manager-Boy.

The bartender, a good-looking blonde with hair about the same length as mine, cocked her head at me. "He's my boss," she said. Then she raised her eyebrows in anticipation of the comeback.

"I'm his daddy," I said, shaking my head so my earring would jingle. I had in the hoop with the dangling guitar. Women love that thing.

She drew the beer, put one in front of me, and slid the other down the bar to Teddy, who was still on the phone. He caught it like a good shortstop and lifted it to his lips. She smiled at his grace, then turned to me. "So. You're him and he's him." She put a CD cover on the bar. One finger tapped a picture of me, then of Teddy.

I tapped the picture of me. As I did, my hand brushed hers. She looked up from the picture. So did I.

You know, Angel, you'd be easier to be faithful to if you weren't fucking dead.

Yes, I know I'm using anger to ease my guilt. No, it's not working.

Either you're going to have to come back to life or I'm going to have to die. This "one on this side, the other on that side" shit isn't working.

Yeah, she came over to our hotel. No, she didn't hook up with Teddy. She was with someone else. . . .

"We're gonna be at the Inn of the Governors later," Teddy said from the end of the bar. It was for the benefit of the bartender, though if he'd looked around at us he'd have seen that he didn't have to say it.

He kept looking out the door and across the lobby and I knew he was communicating with the girl, Brooke, somehow. I didn't figure he could see her, so I guessed he was just standing there being famous. That's pretty much all we ever have to do.

You know, Angel, fame is such bullshit. That girl was a perfectly lovely, intelligent person, someone who helped us, and in return she was being reduced to—what? A bird facing a snake? That's what it feels like much of the time.

Why? Because I have some name and face recognition.

Why? Because I like to make up songs and sing them for people. And so now I'm famous and people pay twenty dollars a pop to watch me do something I'd do for them for free.

Why? So a bunch of assholes can make a living marketing what I do, setting up places for me to do it, taking my picture, writing about my doing it (hell, even Charlie, although I think he saw through it after all), recording my singing and playing.

What's that line from The Byrds' song? "Sell your soul to the company/Who are waiting there to sell plastic ware. . . ."

The bartender leaned over so that her face was close to mine. "Which is your favorite of your albums?"

We looked at each other for about a minute. "*Anthems for Doomed Youth*," I said, telling the truth for once. That's not the one most people, especially most women, want to hear.

"Oh." She leaned back, hesitating, then said, "My favorite is—"

"*How Do You Like Your Blue-Eyed Boys?*" we said together.

She cocked her head and almost smiled. "You know your audience."

"After the fact, maybe," I said. "We were young and looking for love when we wrote that album. We said the things we thought women would want to hear."

"Sounds more like you were looking for sex," she said.

I nodded slightly and looked down at my beer. Smart girl.

"Hey," she said, a little brusquely, sounding so much like you I glanced up at her, startled. "Nothing wrong with that."

We locked eyes then. She had these great hazel eyes. And in early February in Santa Fe, a great tan.

Sometimes need is stronger than love, Angel. It happens. That's why we have forgiveness.

Just then Brooke showed up at the door. "Your ride's here," she said to Teddy, oblivious to the other two people in the bar. The blonde and I broke our gaze and looked at them.

Teddy drained his beer and drew Brooke's eyes to his. "You coming later?" he said.

Brooke didn't say anything. She just kept looking at him. That whole bird and snake thing again.

"She can ride over with me," said the bartender.

We locked eyes again. "Nothing wrong with—" we said together.

"Look," I began.

She reached over and flicked my earring. "I know I like my blue-eyed boy. I just want to know how much." She looked down at the bar then back at me.

I thought hard about you, Angel. I thought hard about me. I thought hard about love, hard about sex, and hard about the difference it makes if you get them together. I thought hard about being dead and being alive.

Then I just thought, *Fuck it*. I mean, sometimes you just have to.

"See you later tonight," I said. I picked up the beer and took a long swig, then handed her the half-full glass.

She took the glass from me and finished off the beer. "For sure."

We nodded at each other that way people do when something's going to happen between them. I turned to follow Teddy out to the Jeep waiting to take us to the Inn of the Governors.

"Hey."

I looked back at her.

"I'm Betsy."

"Yeah. I'm Jay. Jay Breeze."

She held up the CD cover. "I've heard of you."

"Yeah. Right."

Teddy called me and I went out into the snow and joined him for the ride to the hotel.

We ordered lots of food and wine sent up to our suite. The rest of the night went about as you'd expect. The snake got the bird and Betsy found out how much. . . .

It's four o'clock in the morning. Still snowing. I've got a great view out my hotel window of the mountains in the distance. They're the Santa Fe Mountains. I should sleep, I guess, but you know me. It's not going to happen.

I keep looking at the snow coming down, dark shapes of the mountains in the background. Mind if I quote some poetry? "Now more than ever seems it rich to die." John Keats. "Ode to a Nightingale."

Why did you have to die, Angel? Why do you have to be the dead one? I'm the one who's lived dangerously all these years. I'm the one the shrink said had self-destructive tendencies. Why do you have to be the one who left? I never would have left, Angel.

My mother would say (as she said at the time), "John Jay, it's all part of God's plan. We aren't meant to understand. We must accept."

Well, I don't accept, Angel. I'm royally pissed. If God's plan includes killing off twenty-four-year-old girls, then God better get a clue.

Okay. You're right. What do I know? Maybe I should do like the guy in the old song. You wouldn't remember it, but maybe you heard it sometime on one of those oldies stations. It's called "Last Kiss" and goes something like:

Oh where, oh where can my baby be?
The Lord took her away from me.
She's gone to heaven, so I've got to be good,
So I can see my baby when I leave this world. . . .

Doesn't really sound like me, does it? What the

hell, you know? I'd try being good if I thought it would make any difference.

I've been reading a guidebook about the city. Santa Fe means "Holy Faith." I guess it was like that letter I wrote about the dreams. A message. I look for messages from you all the time. In one of our last conversations, one you didn't remember when I asked you about because you were drunk when you called me, you told me that if we were never together again on earth we'd be together in heaven because we were one, and while God might let us be apart here, he'd never have us apart there. I believe that, Angel. I believed you when you told me that. I believe. I have to. It's all I can do.

I've convinced Teddy to let me put that song you mentioned, "Will I See You in Heaven?" on the new album.

It's six in the morning now. Still snowing. I fell asleep for a bit. Dreams of you. They come and come. As always.

The girl? She just left. You'll forgive me for that. Being dead helps you be strong, maybe, but being alive makes you prey to weakness.

I woke up about noon and took a shower, then went to Teddy's room. He was in bed watching TV.

"Wanna order some food?" he asked, scrolling through channels.

"Not me. I'm gonna go down and see what the restaurant is like. You wanna come?"

"Nah. One of us should be in the room in case they call from Albuquerque. Besides, I need a shower." Teddy stopped on a movie channel showing *The Magnificent Ambersons*. "Hey, Orson Welles movie. . . ."

We were singing "The Man Who Broke the Bank at Monte Carlo" as I left to go downstairs.

When I reached the lobby, Paul and Van were standing at the front desk.

February 10, 1992
1:30 A.M.

Angel, I apologize. I've left out a lot again. As usual. Shall I start with where everyone is? Teddy's back in Taos. Mick and Sid went to Phoenix for the next show. Actually, the next show is in Tempe. Mick and Sid are playing in a golf tournament in Phoenix with Alice Cooper. Goddam, we're getting old. And we're too fucking rich. . . .

And Jay? Jay's back in Santa Fe. Inn of the Governors.

We played the Albuquerque show last night (the 8th). We had a two-day layover. One day in Santa Fe—while they got the interstates cleared and we waited for the equipment to arrive—then another in Albuquerque because of a UNM basketball game. So finally, on the 8th, we played the show. . . .

It was an okay show. Ten years ago I would've been pissed at our performance. These days it's all fine. It's hard to have the passion when not a damned thing matters anymore. We're such pros anyway, the audience couldn't tell.

Rich, passionless pros.

"Oh, for a life of sensations rather than of

thoughts!" Keats again.

Why are you the only one who knows what I mean? Why are you the only one who knows who I am? Why do I keep asking a dead woman for the answers to my life's questions? Dammit, Angel, enough already. . . .

Tell you a story: I made Paul drive me back up here after the show. We got in about two in the morning. I had held my room because I knew we had a layover between the University of New Mexico show and the Arizona State University show. So I got Paul a room and we stayed here. It wasn't the same as a few nights ago. Maybe because it wasn't snowing. I sat up for a long while drinking brandy and thinking of you. Couldn't write because the Big Sadness was on me. . . .

The next morning I woke up early (9:30—early for me). Took a quick shower and threw on some clothes, then went down to the restaurant for breakfast. Tried to get through some Huevos Rancheros, but people kept stopping by my table to talk and ask for autographs so the food kept getting cold and I kept sending it back and getting it reheated or ordering more and then the breakfast bill got to be one hundred twenty-five bucks, so I said *fuck it* and took a fresh pot of coffee up to the room. Bought a pack of cigarettes. Smoked a few and drank the coffee. Thought about the autographs. If my count is right I signed fourteen or fifteen. And you wonder why I don't eat. No time . . .

Went by Paul's room and knocked, but he was still asleep. So I decided to take a walk around the Plaza and the Old City.

The hardest part was crossing the lobby. It was

crowded with people going to the ski areas. That's where Teddy was. With the desk clerk, Brooke. She met him there—or was supposed to. So either he's enjoying himself with her or luring some other sweet young thing into his web.

No, I haven't seen Betsy since she left my room early that morning. And I didn't come back here to see her. I just liked it and needed a little time away from the guys.

Yeah, I know. The lobby. See, I didn't have anyone to walk through with. That's what it was.

It's different when Teddy's along. He knows he's a Rock Star. He believes in his heart of hearts that he deserves to be who he is. You go somewhere with Teddy and he just mesmerizes everyone because he knows how to be famous.

Or if I'm with Mick or Sid it's okay because they have so much fun that I end up having fun, too. They just laugh about it all.

Paul, Van, and Scott protect me, of course. That's their job. They make me feel important and separate.

But no one was with me.

While I was standing there working up the nerve to walk across the lobby and just deal with it (as Mick says), I started thinking about this poem from *Alice in Wonderland*. The one about the mice. Do you know it?

> We lived beneath the mat
> Warm and snug and fat
> But one woe, & that
> Was the cat!
> To our joys a clog,
> To our eyes a fog,

On our hearts a log,
Was the dog!

What happens in the end is that the mice get
squashed by the cat and dog who are hunting a rat.
Jay, what are you getting at? (I hear your voice saying
that so clearly.) I think I mean this: I think I wanted
to live beneath the mat, but that's not how it turned
out for me.

I became something else. The dog or the cat. I'd
like to think the dog, but I'm pretty sure I'm the cat—
they're so conscious of where they step. I'm trying not
to squash any of the mice, and I'm very afraid when I
walk through a crowd that I'll ignore someone whose
heart is in their hands and held toward me—which is
the worst kind of squashing.

So I like to have someone with me. Maybe just to
deflect responsibility, now that I think about it.

Finally I walked through the lobby. I did a Queen
Elizabeth, you know? I walked through and smiled
and waved at everyone and hoped I hadn't ignored
anyone who might have cared about getting a smile or
a wave from me.

I did my best, Angel.

You think I take all this too seriously, don't you?

It was a gorgeous day, sunny but cold as hell.
Wonder why we say that? Maybe it's from Milton.
He's the one who talks about "darkness visible."

Maybe the flames of hell are bitter cold.

Santa Fe is beautiful. The snow on all the
Spanish buildings felt strange to me, though. I guess
I've watched too many Westerns. Big John Wayne fan.
You know me. I kept thinking it should be sunny and

hot. The snow threw me off.

I wandered around, going in and out of shops. Got you some things: a beautiful silver-and-turquoise barrette and a matching bracelet. I'll put them away in a drawer with the other things I've bought for you. I know, I know—I'm crazy. But I couldn't imagine the barrette anywhere but in that blonde mane of yours. . . .

And they led me to Anthony.

What happened was this: I was walking up some side street, still looking for things for you, just admiring the city and thinking about what to get you. (Yeah, stupid, maybe, but I'm doing the best I can. You're not the one having to live this out alone. . . .)

Well, I looked up and I was at a street corner. And there in front of me was the Plaza. So I went hiking through there and across the way I could see the Palace of the Governors. So I went there. Well, out in front of the museum (which is what it is now) sat all these Navajo artisans with their wares spread out on really cool blankets. So I started wandering back and forth looking at all the jewelry. Because it was so cold, there were only two other people shopping—a couple about seven, eight years younger than I. They kept looking at me then whispering to each other.

Well, you know how I can be. But I went over to them and smiled and said, "Yeah, it's me."

Angel, the woman was so happy. She just clutched at her husband's coat and whispered, "Jay Breeze" again and again. Real fanatic, you know? The kind I always like.

Her husband and I chatted a bit. Then suddenly the woman blurts out, "Excuse me," and takes off across the Plaza. The husband (I think his name was

Phil—I never remember last names, to protect myself) shrugged and kept chatting. He asked the usual questions and I gave the usual answers.

Then suddenly the wife came scampering back across the Plaza waving something. When she got to us she unfurled this poster of The Lost Generation. It was one of the first ever done of us, from 1975 or so. I have a framed copy in my music room downstairs. It's the one of us standing in the doorway of Mick's old apartment. Everybody's looking directly at the camera except me—I'm just sort of looking off into the distance. Up in the right-hand corner is a paraphrase of the Gertrude Stein quote: "We are all The Lost Generation . . ."

"I paid forty-five dollars for it," she said shyly. "There's this great little shop on Water Street that has posters and art. I didn't even dicker with them. Phil and I saw it this morning. It was all over town that you and Teddy Hatter were here a couple of days ago in the big snowstorm. We saw your show in Dallas. We had fourth-row seats. . . ." Suddenly she put her hand over her mouth as if she'd said too much. Her husband and I looked at each other and smiled, he sheepishly, I—well, I smiled sheepishly, too.

"Would you like me to autograph this?" I asked quietly.

She nodded, hand still over her mouth.

I checked my pockets. Nothing to write with. The husband and wife started looking, too. Nothing . . .

That's when Anthony appeared.

This whole exchange had taken place in front of his jewelry arrangement. I suppose he'd sat there the whole time watching. Then, when I needed his help, he appeared beside me with a felt-tipped pen.

"Thanks," I said. He caught my eye as I took the pen.

He nodded solemnly and disappeared from my line of sight.

"How shall I sign the poster?" I asked the woman.

"To Lisa," she whispered.

"To Phil, too?" He and I smiled at each other.

"Make it to Lisa," he said.

I signed the poster to both of them, rolled it up carefully, and handed it to Lisa. She clutched it to her chest and whispered, "Thank you, Jay Breeze" two or three times.

Phil and I shook hands then, and he led her away. She glanced back several times. Each time I waved. When she got about fifty feet away, she handed him the poster and ran back to me.

I was ready for her. I held out my arms and she flew into them. I kissed her on the cheek. She hugged my neck tightly. I pried her loose and sent her back to Phil. He'd walked about half the way back to us. When she started toward him he waved kind of diffidently at me. I held up my hand in a sort of half-apologetic/half-benedictory gesture meant to say, "It happens. Don't let it bother you. She'll be okay."

Yeah, I know. Playing the Rock Star . . .

I think I do it because it's the only time now I can let a woman touch me while I'm sober without getting the creeps.

It makes them so happy.

Yeah, it makes me happy, too, Angel.

I love you, too.

When Phil and Lisa were gone, I turned to the guy who'd given me the pen. I still had it in my hand.

I returned it to him with a word of thanks. He nodded again. Then he just sat there behind his array of jewelry.

There was something to his nodding. I didn't know quite what to make of it, so I knelt and scanned his jewelry. That's when he asked the question: "How do you do it, man?"

That, Angel, is *the* question. Not, "What made you do it?" or, "How long can you do it?" or even, "Why do you do it?" Those questions you can be flip or philosophical about as it suits you.

I've been dreading for ten years that someone would ask me *this* question. Wait a minute. I'm not making myself clear. Sure, I've been asked that question before. But it was always in the context of surviving touring or something like that.

"What's your name?" I asked. I was stalling.

"Anthony LaPlaca."

I even remember his last name.

"I'm Jay Breeze." I offered my hand. He shook hands with me, but only as if he were honoring some foreign gesture, like kissing cheeks in France.

"You sure are." He looked off toward where Lisa and Phil had disappeared. "That was remarkable, man."

I shrugged. "Business as usual."

He looked back at me. "It must be hard for you. You have so many choices. How do you do it?"

I didn't answer right away, Angel. I couldn't.

Was he asking how I deal with being a rock star? What do I tell him—that all the money, all the women, all the booze and dope in the world wouldn't change your being dead? That I've spent the last two or three years doing little good deeds to try and make up for some of the awful shit I did during the previous fifteen? That being able to have anyone won't make you want them? That it's somehow harder to be Lewis Carroll's cat than one of his mice?

"I don't think I get what you mean," I said.

He didn't say anything for a while. He just sat there and looked off across the Plaza. I began scanning his wares again. That's when I found the barrette and bracelet. They weren't exactly the same, but they matched each other. I know that sounds crazy, so I'll explain it this way and you'll understand—they were like you and me. . . .

"It must be great to be able to do this," I said, holding first the barrette, then the bracelet up to the light. The silver gleamed and the turquoise flashed. Or maybe the other way . . .

"I do a little thing. The land gives me the silver and turquoise. I shape them and polish them and sell them here so that I may live and you may see what the land can do."

"It doesn't seem like a little thing to me." I put the barrette and the bracelet beside each other on the blanket, away from the other pieces. They were beautiful. Hell, they were perfect. Their differences only made them right together.

Yeah, I'm being self-indulgent, Angel. I'm a rock star. It's what we do.

I could feel him watching me patiently, so I looked up. "What I do is a little thing," he said. "I'm tied to the land. It is a good thing, but it is little. You—you do a big thing." He nodded again. That damned nod . . .

I looked again at the pieces. "Being able to take what the land offers and make things so beautiful seems like a big thing to me."

His response was remarkable, Angel.

He picked up the barrette and fingered it, then laid it down and did the same with the bracelet. "These are good work." He put the bracelet down and we admired both pieces. Then he shook his head. "But they are small things. Your songs—those are big things."

He said nothing more. I looked up at him. He was watching me. "I sense that you do not believe me, and this troubles me. When I watched you with that couple, at first I was impressed by what seemed to be your modesty. But as you talked with the man, and then the woman, I realized that your modesty was not modesty based on understanding the big thing that you do and being humbled by it, but instead was a false belief that your work is not important and is modesty based on a kind of mistaken sense of shame."

He had me, Angel.

"My work is of the land," he said earnestly, looking directly into my eyes. "We can touch it and see it. It is even beautiful," he said lovingly, touching the bracelet again. Then he looked at me and spoke again. "Your work is of the spirit, Jay Breeze. It comes from the sky. We cannot touch it, but we hear it and feel it and it makes us see things in our hearts and minds."

It was my turn to smile and look away. I gazed across the Plaza. Some people were coming out of a shop across the way. One of them pointed over at us and grabbed another by the arm. Word was out.

"Your songs, my friend, are big things," he added, bringing my attention back to him. "They are like whispers from the spirits."

Way cool, huh, Angel?

"Listen," I said, kneeling on the edge of the blanket and picking up the bracelet, "what you say—I mean—wow. You know?"

We both smiled. I guess at the insightfulness of our generation so poetically expressed.

I found myself trying to tell him about you, then, Angel. It seemed like the thing to do. It was hard to talk about you. I can't tell people what I feel. It would make no sense. So I just babbled about you, about us, about anything but your . . . death. . . .

He reached over and grasped my arm. "You are mistaken, my friend. She has not left you. Even death will not take her away. She is here with us now. When you need her, just be still. Her love will come to you. Yours will go to her. Just be still."

We sat in silence. I closed my eyes and tried to be still. And faintly, faintly, but truly, I began to feel your love come to me, Angel. Thank you . . .

I opened my eyes. Anthony was looking at me. "She came to you?"

"She came."

"She will always come, Jay Breeze. Even when the world presses in on you, the crowds hurting or frightening you with their strange ideas of love, she will come if you are still."

I grabbed him by the shoulders. "How did you know this? I don't doubt you. I just want it to be true—you know?"

"It is true." He made no effort to move me away.

That's when I started to cry.

"It is true for you," he said quietly, not ignoring my crying, accepting it, "because this is how we know things. You know love through her. Love never leaves us. Because for you she is love, she can never leave you. You should go to her. You need her. She completes your soul."

"She's dead." I don't know how I got the words out. It was like someone else's voice said it, and I really heard it for the first time.

Anthony leaned back against the wall of the museum, pulling away from my grasp. I looked at him. He sat for several minutes, eyes closed. Then he reached over and picked up the bracelet and barrette and held them out. "For her."

We looked at each other for what seemed like a long time. Then I took the jewelry and put it into my coat pocket.

"Be careful, Jay Breeze," he said, looking away, across the Plaza.

"You bet. As always." I smiled, but he didn't look at me again. I waited a few moments, then got to my feet and headed for the hotel.

Later that day I sent Paul on an errand. He went to the bank and got a few thousand dollars, then went to the museum and found Anthony and bought all his jewelry. I'll give it as Christmas presents or something. . . .

Maybe we're not too rich after all.

Love,

Jay

JAY'S BOOK OF DAYS

The secret ministry of frost.
(Coleridge)

I think I hate money.

Move confidently toward your dreams. Live the life you've imagined.
(Thoreau)

When I meet a woman whose first reaction isn't, "Wow, you're a rock star," I'm going to marry her.
(Mick Norris)

I would like for someone to see me.

The reason everyone else in any given rock band at any given time thinks the drummer is nuts is because he is.
(Teddy Hatter)

Every day is like every other day except for its differences.
(Sid Vegas)

I want to believe in love, but I'm heterosexual.
(Mick Norris)

Everyday I write the book.
(Elvis Costello)

And then there are people in music who write things

like the Taco Bell jingles. So, listen to Mozart, then listen to a Taco Bell jingle. And tell me there's no high and low art.

Times reporter George Superior—"Mr. Norris, I think what *my* readers want to know is, how is it that a man like yourself—a clearly intelligent man—a man with at least some college education from a good school—would choose to wear your hair to your shoulders, dress in blue jeans, women's blouses and velvet jackets, and play rock music at hearing-damaging volumes?"

Mick—"Well, you know, George, the money's good, I get to work in the exciting field of electronics, I don't have to wear Brooks Brothers suits—oh, and I get to f*** great-looking women. Why'd you become a reporter?"
(from the *NY Times* column "Superior Opinions")

It's comforting to know that there are some things I won't do.

What I really need to learn is how *not to* be lonely.

At Bay

Dear Angel,

This is about how the tour ended.

You know how the tour ended.

The debacle in San Francisco.

Here's the thing about San Francisco: it's the most fucked-up city in the world.

I don't mean to imply that I disapprove of being fucked up. I don't.

But I've had enough of going everywhere and doing everything to last a lifetime. And San Francisco—well, it's San Francisco.

It's all hills and the hills are tall, and there's the bay, but that's on the wrong side all the time and besides it's full of sharks, and there's Alcatraz and—I don't know, Angel, maybe it was that I was tired, maybe it was that it was the end of the tour and I always get depressed at the end of a tour, maybe it was looking around at the rest of the band, Teddy and Mick and Sid, and then at Paul and Scott and all the other support guys who've worked with us and for us for the last—Jesus Christ—twenty years (!) and realizing that we're not kids anymore, that we're men, and not young men, either, that we're all about forty, and that all we've ever done is be born and grow up a little and go to school and play music and be rich and famous and—

No. You're right. It's not about that. It's about

Ralph Dodge.

Okay. It's about death.

It's about Ralph's death—and your death.

It's about wanting to know why these people I love are dead and I'm not.

But I think we've got to start with San Francisco.

So we fly up from L.A. I hate doing that.

I mean, really. Why have the Pacific Coast Highway if you're not going to use it?

So we fly up to San Fran and we get to the airport and for some reason there's a press conference and MTV is there and the *SF Enquirer* has somehow gotten Hunter Thompson to show up for God's sake.

There's also some asshole reporter from Much Music TV in Canada who thinks he'll make a bit of a name for himself as a music reporter by cornering one of us and asking mean-spirited questions about the delays putting out the new album and he, out of dumb luck, corners Mick, who's the reason the album's not out because he has to re-record some vocals at Geffen's personal request and feels like shit about it, so when this stupid little reporter starts hammering at him, Mick just loses it and cleans the guy's clock.

I mean he punches the hell out of the poor guy.

And screws up his right hand in the process.

And while this is going on, the MTV people panic and Hunter pulls a gun and the airport cops and some city cops show up and pretty soon we're all going off to jail.

Then we're sitting in a holding cell with Hunter Thompson and he looks over at me and says, "Jay, where the hell is Charlie Beagle?"

"Chapel Hill, Hunter. Where I ought to be," I say.

"What the hell's he doing in Chapel Hill?"

"He's a fucking journalism professor at UNC, Hunter. You know that."

"Well, he ought to be covering this tour," Hunter says.

"Why?" I ask.

"Because then I wouldn't be sitting in a goddam jail cell with a bunch of aging pretty boy rock stars waiting for my editor to come bail me out. I'd be investigating neural gas tests they're conducting at the underground facilities in the Rockies west of Colorado Springs."

I love Hunter. He actually cares about something.

Meanwhile, Mick's hand is starting to swell. And it's getting more painful by the second. And we have a show in four hours.

We're doing two shows at the Cow Palace and we're done.

"February 15 and 16 at San Francisco's Cow Palace. See the last of the Romantics! The Lost Generation's farewell shows from the 'Lovely, Dark, and Deep' tour—"

The heavy door outside shuts and we hear no more of the radio announcement. There's a vague sound of footsteps and then the door is unlocked and in strolls a guard with a harried-looking suit who can't be more than thirty.

"Who the hell are you?" Hunter growls.

The suit identifies himself as a lawyer for the *Enquirer*. He tells Hunter he's there to bail him out.

Hunter doesn't say anything else. He just gets up

and walks past the lawyer and the jailer and he's gone.

"It's nice to know some things never change." Teddy walks over to the cell door and looks out. The jailer edges over as if to prevent his escape.

Teddy looks at him and laughs. "Yeah, you better watch me, Barney. I was gonna bust outta here and make that show down at the Cow Palace. If I'd gotten by you, I'd have walked right out of here and attracted no notice."

Teddy's wearing cream-and-burgundy two-toned shoes, jeans with holes in the knees, a "Mr. Yuck" T-shirt, and a woman's silk jacket—lilac-colored. His hair, shoulder-length and dark brown, has a pale pink streak at his widow's peak.

I know, Angel, I hear you. Rock stars do dress in silly clothes. But we like them.

"Listen, officer, I hate to bug you, but my hand is getting pretty painful and we've got a show to do tonight. Is there anybody here who could look at it?"

We're all taken aback. Mick's tone is so conciliatory, so respectful, we know he must really be hurt. Sid, Teddy, and I look at each other. There'll be no show tonight.

It's the closing of the circle. Teddy, Sid, and I have all caused cancellations before. Only Mick never has. We've always joked that if Mick ever caused us to cancel we'd break up the band.

I look at Teddy and he at me. We're both thinking the same thing. *This is it. This is the end. Really the end. Just like The Beatles, we're finishing up for good in fucking San Francisco.*

In the next instant, I realize that Mick and Sid are both looking at us and that they're thinking the same thing. *It's over. Twenty-one years and it's over.*

You can imagine what the mood was like in that cell, Angel. Not the happiest bunch of campers at the jamboree right then.

We've pretty much ignored the suit, and he's still standing there. "Are you getting us out, too?" Mick asks hopefully.

"No, I'm sorry Mr. Norris; you and Mr. Hatter and Mr. Vegas and Mr. Breeze are going to have to stay here for a bit." He looks at Mick. "I will have a doctor here immediately to tend to your hand." He turns and motions the guard forward. When the guy steps away from the door, Teddy feints as if to dart through it. The guard starts to jump back, then smiles sheepishly at Teddy, who smiles indulgently back at him.

The lawyer whispers something and the guard leaves. He looks at Teddy, smiles sheepishly again, and leaves the cell door open. "The guard will be back shortly with a doctor," he says.

He takes a deep breath, looks at the floor, then back at the three of us he can see. "Mr. Hatter, could you step over here, please?"

This is not good. It's never good when official people ask for your attention, Angel. When they called me from the hospital the night of your wreck, they asked me to sit down, they had something to tell me. I knew then you were dead, sweetness. It's never good.

Teddy moves over and takes a seat on the bench by me.

"Gentlemen, Mr. Geffen will be here in a little while to pick you up. I have already arranged your release. I'm sorry I deceived you a moment ago—"

Imagine that, we all think, as we look back and

forth at each other. *Deceived by a lawyer. But why's David coming?*

Well, Angel, I'd be twice as rich if it weren't for lawyers. That's why I feel this way.

Yes, I know, I'm rich enough as it is.

"Gentlemen, about an hour ago—" He stops.

This is really going to be bad.

"About an hour ago," he continues in a somber voice, "a plane carrying Ralph Dodge, U.S. Air Force pilot and astronaut, went down in a wooded area northwest of Brunswick, Georgia. He'd met with a governmental group there and was on his way to Atlanta to speak to students at the Georgia Institute of Technology. Major Dodge was killed in the crash."

Teddy and I look at each other. Ralph had grown up with Teddy and Charlie. Mick, Sid, and I had gotten to be friends with him while we were still in college.

He was such a cool guy. Charlie had done a story on our visit with him in Florida during the 1978 tour. "Two Kinds of Star Power," he'd called it.

Ralph was the real thing, Angel. I mean, Ralph flew the space shuttle. That's worth something. That's not just playing little pop songs for ridiculous sums of money and vandalizing Holiday Inns. Flying the space shuttle, that's something. That's heroic. And if you'd have shown people on the street pictures of Teddy, Charlie, and Ralph, lots of them would recognize Teddy (or me or any other rock star), some would recognize Charlie (or Hunter Thompson), but almost nobody would recognize Ralph.

What the hell's the matter with us, Angel?

Another really big thing, Angel. It was Ralph who pulled me out of the water when I jumped off Jimmy

Buffett's boat that time. If he hadn't done that, I'd have drowned and never known you and understood what it is to love someone.

He was a hero. Professionally and personally. That's all I can say about the guy.

Teddy signals for the huddle. We all huddle together before every performance—and occasionally in times of crisis. The guys huddled in the emergency room with me the night you—

"Okay," says Teddy, "we've gotta think what we need to do. We've lost a good friend. We'll need to check on Valerie and their daughter. Then—"

He started to break, so I took over. "We need to call Charlie. He probably already knows, but we want to let him know we're thinking of him. And we'll need to get Paul and Scott to schedule a flight back to Florida for the funeral—"

The doctor came in. Sid looked up, out of the huddle, and said, "Okay, let's get Mick's hand fixed."

We separated and the doctor took Mick over to a bench and examined him. He turned Mick's hand over several times, touching it in various places. Mick visibly winced each time he did.

I went over and put my hand on Mick's shoulder. When he looked up at me, I could see the tears slipping down his cheeks. His hand was as fucked up as San Francisco.

And that was the end. The lawyer had disappeared when we went into the huddle. He came back then and told us that we were released. The doctor told Mick he needed to go to a hospital and get his hand set. Mick told him that he needed to go to Florida. We settled on going to the doctor's office a few blocks from the police station. He set Mick's hand with a temporary cast and made him swear to get to a hospital when we arrived in Florida.

All this happened after.

I haven't told you about the scene as we left the police station.

We came walking out, rock stars dressed in rock star clothes, Sid leading the way, Mick cradling his hand as if it were a piece of Limoges ware, Teddy and me side by side, heads down, ignoring everyone.

Some of the cops started clapping.

We looked up and there were maybe twenty people in the room—mostly cops, but a few of the sundry types one would expect to see in a big city police station.

And the rest of the crowd picked up on the cops' clapping and then everybody in the room was clapping and David Geffen was in the room and two or three assistants and they were herding us out to a limo and the cops started cheering as well as clapping and Teddy and I waved to them the way we've waved at crowd after crowd after crowd after crowd over the last seventeen years we've been famous.

And then we were outside.

And there was the reporter—the little shit who tried to bully Mick—and he's looking the worse for wear (a black eye and a clear bruise on his cheek), and he comes up to us, a camera guy behind him, and I felt Teddy tense up and I was thinking, *This sumbitch has a death wish* and Teddy and Sid started for him but he ignored them and stepped up to Mick.

"I'm sorry for your loss, Mr. Norris—really, for all of you. I hope everything turns out all right. I just came down here to see the charges against you dropped." He nodded his head at each of us.

And he held out his hand to Mick.

Mick just looked at him for a moment, a little dazed. (The doctor gave him some pretty sweet painkillers that he took before we left the cell. They were just kicking in.)

Then he held up the broken hand.

The reporter looked at it. After a second, he realized it was broken.

"Oh, man," he said, "I fucked up the show."

Mick released his broken hand and put his left hand on the kid's shoulder. "We wouldn't have played, anyway. Not after finding out about Ralph."

Teddy, Sid, and I all stopped right there and looked at each other. Mick was right.

We were still The Lost Generation.

See what I mean about San Francisco being so fucked up? We couldn't even get right why the tour was ending.

So there I was in a Lear Jet whisking across America to help bury the best guy in our crowd.

And I'm wondering about stuff like, what did Ralph think of in those last moments and what did you think of in those last moments and did you think of me in those last moments and would I think of you in those last moments.

And I'm wondering if we'll make up those Cow Palace dates although I know we won't.

And I'm wondering if The Lost Generation will ever play another show.

This is the way the world ends, Angel.

Not with a bang—just in confusion.

Love,
Jay

(Another Editor's Note: These are all the letters Jay wrote—or at least all that I could retrieve. There was a corrupted file, a letter written from Chapel Hill about six months after the others. But that's all there is to tell about it.

But there was this—a story Jay wrote about something that happened—actually to me and Teddy. This was in the period when the band was going through lots of drummers. Sid hadn't come along yet and Teddy was despairing that he'd never get the band going. We all know how that turned out.

I must've said any number of times when we talked about this over the years that I should write about it.

Jay did.

I think it says a lot about Jay.

And probably too much about me and Teddy.

For entirely different reasons.)

Fat Annie

Annie got to be friends with Jill and Sally, then, by extension, the guys in the band. All the guys—Roger, Tom, Larry, and Bill—got to know Annie. They all thought she was very kind and jolly.

"Call me Fat Annie," she said to them the first time she met them. "Everybody does."

Annie went to all the band's shows once she got to know them. She always cheered after every song. She certainly seemed jolly.

After the shows were over, Roger and Tom would go off with their girlfriends Jill and Sally. Annie would stay at the club or bar and slowly drink one beer. Larry and Bill would drink several each. Annie would then drive them home in her car.

After a while, they began not to go directly back to Larry and Bill's apartment. They went to private places outside town, parking on old farm roads and talking. Soon they had a favorite place, a small abandoned farm on a hill overlooking the city. Annie would pull the car into the farmyard. They would crawl out onto the hood of the car, lie back against the windshield, and consider life. Larry and Annie would often talk for hours. Bill didn't say much, and sometimes he fell asleep. Mostly he listened.

Annie treasured these times, although she never told Larry and Bill.

Once Larry and Bill got drunk before a show because they were frustrated with Roger and Tom's lack of ambition. Annie had to go to their apartment and pick them up to get them to the show. This happened a couple of times. They established a pattern. Annie would come to the guys' apartment on the afternoon of a show to discourage them from drinking too much. She would then drive them to the club or bar. After, they would go to the farm and talk.

Larry rode in the front seat with Annie. Bill rode in the back with the guitars.

One of the things they often talked about was the band's future. Larry and Bill were frustrated with Roger and Tom's willingness to settle for playing small clubs and bars. Larry and Bill wanted bigger things. They wanted to make records and play big concerts and become rich rock stars.

Annie never laughed at their dreams. They didn't seem hopeless or far-fetched to her. She had dreams of her own. The fact that Larry and Bill had dreams made her feel close to them. She liked that feeling.

Annie's dreams were about more than losing weight. While she knew she was not obese, she also knew that she was overweight. She had begun calling herself Fat Annie in high school as a defense against the cruel treatment she had received in junior high and expected to receive in high school. When she said it first, it seemed she controlled it.

Then, after a while, being Fat Annie became a role for her. She found herself able to separate from the character—the loud, jolly do-gooder who did things like chauffeur around drunk, small-time rock musicians because any man's company was better than none—and Anne, the woman of substance who quietly wrote and published poetry and who planned to finish college, diet and exercise hard for two years, and get a job with a small college publisher until she could earn her MFA in writing, build a career as a poet, and get a job teaching at a little liberal arts college somewhere and marry a professor, preferably one who taught history.

Annie was really quite pretty. She had auburn hair, green eyes, and what used to be called a Cupid's-bow mouth. Her complexion was smooth and fair.

Larry and Bill were both good-looking themselves. Larry was tall and slender in the best rock star tradition with dark, shaggy hair and eyes a bluish-gray that approximated slate. His strong features reflected his English heritage. Bill was slender also, but slightly shorter than Larry. His mop of dirty blond hair never seemed to be combed, but somehow it suited his nearly angelic features. He also had blue eyes, but his were of the brighter variety and glittered when he drank, which was too often for his own good.

They were good-looking kids with talent and dreams and not enough experience with life.

After several months of the pattern, Bill decided it was time to have a talk with Larry about Annie. They were having a few beers and watching a baseball game one Saturday afternoon in late April. The semester was almost over and school would be out soon.

Bill felt that Larry should make some decision about Annie before she made plans for the summer. He and Larry planned to quit the band with Roger and Tom and join a new band with two guys named Mike and Tony. Tony's brother was an agent who had promised them better bookings as well as a chance at touring. That meant they might not come back to school in the fall—or ever. Bill thought that it would be better if he and Larry made a clean break with Annie to minimize hurt feelings. Bill had decent instincts.

"So. What about Fat Annie?" Bill asked that afternoon, lying on the sofa. The Braves were down six runs to the Mets.

"What do you mean?" Larry asked from the overstuffed chair. He knew Bill well enough to know what he was asking, but he hated to deal with complications, even when he knew he should. Larry wanted a simple life, an uncluttered life. Being a rock star appealed to him at least partially because he would always be traveling, always moving away from any trouble that might arise.

"Do you think she's in love with you?" Bill twisted his neck to look directly at Larry.

"That's crazy." Larry turned away from Bill and threw his legs across the arm of the chair. "We're good friends. We like to talk," he continued, more to himself than to Bill.

Bill sat up and put his beer on the coffee table. He watched and waited until Larry capitulated and turned toward him. "You talk half the night away. Sometimes you talk about crazy, stupid things. And sometimes," he stopped and took a pull of the beer, "you both forget I'm there. Doesn't that mean anything?"

Larry leaned forward in his chair. He rested his elbows on his knees and propped his chin in his hands. "I don't know what it means, Bill. It bothers me."

"How do *you* feel about *her*?"

Larry shrugged. "She's a great girl. She's smart, she's fun, she's even pretty—" He stopped when he saw Bill's arched eyebrows. "You know what I mean," he continued halfheartedly.

Bill nodded. He thought Annie was pretty, too.

But he knew that the girls he saw on TV, in movies, and in magazines that he thought were sexy were slender.

Suddenly, he thought of a way to help his friend.

"You've got to tell her . . ." Bill began.

"I can't tell her that—" Larry put his face in his hands. This was going to be complicated and he hated it.

"I don't mean that," Bill continued. "You can't tell her it's because—you know. You've got to tell her that we're quitting Roger and Tom and Good for Nothing and joining up with Tony and Mike to form The Lost Souls. That's what you've got to do."

Larry considered. It *was* a way out. Still, somehow it didn't seem right. But he had learned, as so many have, that while lying might not be right, it made life a lot easier. He thought of Annie and how her voice sounded cool and comfortable in the darkness and how her hand felt good to his touch.

And he decided that Bill was right. It was better to lie. And then he'd be gone, and that trouble would be behind him.

"I'll talk to Annie tonight," he said aloud.

"Good man." Bill nodded without looking at him. "Now. How about another beer?" he asked, rising from the sofa.

"Good man."

As Bill went off to the kitchen, Larry rehearsed what he would say to Annie. Everything he tried felt self-serving. He remembered a line he'd read somewhere: "He was unforgettable in a crummy kind of way." He suddenly realized Annie would remember him that way.

Then a Braves batter hit a grand slam homer and

he was distracted from his troubles for a while.

Larry and Bill's leaving the band to join up with Tony and Mike became moot that night. Roger and Jill came by as Larry and Bill were waiting for Annie to take them to dinner.

"We wanted you to know first—well, after Sally and Tom," said Jill, waving her left hand. There was no mistaking the diamond ring on her finger. "We're getting married in August."

Roger stood just behind her looking at Larry and Bill both sheepishly and defiantly. If those two wanted to waste their lives trying to be rock stars, he thought, well, they were their lives to waste. He would get his marketing degree in two weeks and he already had a job with an insurance company selling financial plans. He and Jill would get married in August. He was all set.

"We're having an engagement party Friday night," Jill said. "You cancelled your gig at the Carousel Club, didn't you, Roger? Anyway, we have to go. I need to meet Sally to plan for the party. And Roger, you and Tom need to get your equipment out of your apartment." She threw the door open and strode out.

"So I guess you're leaving the band," Larry said sarcastically.

"Looks that way." Roger tried to smile at him; he sneered instead. He disliked Larry's dedication to music. It made *his* pragmatism feel small.

Larry and Bill looked at each other. "That's a shame," they said simultaneously, insincerely.

Roger turned on his heel and stalked out after Jill. As the door closed behind him, Larry and Bill burst into laughter.

Annie picked up Larry and Bill and drove them to the engagement party. The festivities lasted long into the night, but Larry, Bill, and Annie drank little. Sometime late in the evening Larry and Bill told a joke about the astronauts in the Challenger explosion. Several of the people present were offended. Roger's hair stylist called Larry a drunken swine. Bill had to hold Larry back to keep him from hitting the guy.

Roger tried to smooth things over. He climbed onto the coffee table and spoke to the group. "Let's let bygones be bygones," he said.

People continued to mutter.

He looked over at Larry and Bill. They waggled upheld beer bottles at him and looked contemptuous. He sniffed and looked at the rest of the group. "Say," he continued, "Jill and I want to thank you all for coming tonight and making our engagement party such a success."

People applauded and cheered.

Flushed with success, he continued. "I guess we'll be having more of these parties soon."

People looked at each other questioningly.

"Why, I bet Tom and Sally will be having one of these parties before the summer's gone," he went on. He looked at them. Sally blushed and leaned against Tom who waggled a finger at him good-naturedly. It had become an open secret at the party that they planned to marry in December. Tom was going to work in his dad's car dealership after graduating in August.

People cheered and applauded again.

Roger looked about the room and felt gratified by the reaction. He noticed Larry and Bill leaning against the far wall, looking sullen. In the flush of alcohol and applause he felt a flash of wit. "And I'll bet," he said, "that before the year is out we might even have one of these parties for Larry and Fat Annie!"

He looked at Jill, but she was not smiling. Then he saw Annie standing just behind Jill looking horrified. He looked at Larry and Bill. Larry looked at him as if he wanted to kill him.

Annie suddenly charged across the room and out the door, knocking people out of her way as she went. Larry and Bill dashed after her.

They caught up to her in the parking lot of the apartment complex. She was standing by her car, trembling as she tried to unlock the door. Larry took the keys from her gently and opened the car. He pulled forward the front seat and motioned toward the backseat. "Get in, Annie," he said.

She looked at him for a moment, then crawled into the car. Larry turned and tossed the keys to Bill. "Drive, Bill." He got into the backseat with Annie. Bill flipped the front seat back, got in, and drove.

They stopped at a convenience store at the edge of town. Bill went in and bought a sackful of beer. Then he drove them out to the farm.

When they got there, Bill took the sack of beer and got out of the car. Larry and Annie followed. Bill put the beer onto the car roof then climbed up beside it. He lay on his back looking at the sky.

Larry and Annie crawled onto the hood and lay back against the windshield. Annie leaned her head against Larry's shoulder. He put his arm about her. They looked up at the stars.

"This is nice," Annie said quietly.

"Yes, it is." Larry patted Annie on the arm.

They were quiet for a long time. Bill tried to count the stars in the Little Dipper.

"Why don't you talk?" Bill said suddenly, speaking to the night sky.

Larry and Annie looked at each other. They began to talk in low voices. Bill strained to hear what they said.

"I don't think Roger meant to be cruel," said Larry.

"I know, but he didn't have to say anything at all," Annie replied.

"He was drunk, Annie."

"They all were. But no one else said anything like that."

"Roger was the one talking."

They were silent for a time.

"I suppose you're right," Annie said finally. "Anyone could have said it."

"Anyone."

"There are seventeen stars in the Little Dipper," said Bill.

"That's good." Annie and Larry smiled at each other.

Everyone counted stars for a while.

"Larry, can I ask you something?" Annie said finally.

Larry shifted on the car's hood and took his arm from around her shoulders. "Maybe." He took a long drink of beer.

Everything was quiet. Finally Annie said softly, so softly that Larry had to struggle to hear, "I love you, Larry. Do you love me?"

Larry didn't answer.

"I said, 'Do you—'"

"I heard you." Larry drained his beer can, then sat up and threw it toward an old pond down the hill from the farmyard.

"Shouldn't throw the cans around like that," said Bill. "Trying not to fuck up the world."

"The world's fucked up already." Larry leaned forward and put his face in his hands.

Annie tumbled off the hood. "I'll go get the can." She started toward the pond.

"I'll come with you." Bill swung around to get off the roof.

"No," said Annie. She moved away at a stumbling trot. "I'll get the can and come right back. Besides I need to be alone—to be excused."

Annie sped up as she moved down the hill toward the pond. By the time she reached the water's edge, she was at a full run. The grass was wet and the shore slippery. Annie lost her footing and fell.

Sprawled on the ground she clutched at the grass. She started to cry. To make herself stop, she rubbed her face against the turf, harder and harder, so hard that she uprooted grass. Finally, she cried herself out and fell asleep.

After a while, Larry and Bill got concerned because Annie didn't come back. They went down to the pond and found her. They tried to see if she was hurt. Bill knelt beside her. "Annie, are you all right?"

Annie snorted and sniffled but did not answer.

"What do we do now?" Bill asked Larry.

"Take her home."

They woke Annie and helped her back to the car. Larry helped clean her face. They drove back to the city, Larry and Bill in front, Annie in the back, alone.

Jay Breeze, 1991

(Yet Another Editor's Note: What follows are fragments—the detritus that doesn't fit anywhere else. In no particular order, here's what I've been able to cobble together: There's obvious shit like a discography, some sample lyrics [I just chose one song I like from each of the albums], and an interview I did with Teddy and Jay in 1977 for *Rolling Stone*. The interview is significant because it was the first public revelation of Jay Breeze's son Jakob who lives in Frankfurt, Germany, with his mother Marlene Bergen, a noted sculptor. There's a fragment of a profile I worked on for *RS* about Jay that was never published—and that I now realize I should have finished, and maybe will someday when working on it doesn't make me feel so damned bad. There are some more pieces from "Jay's Book of Days"—from a section he once laughingly described to me as a project called, "The-Rock-and-Roll Handbook." And finally, obits for Jay and Angel [I've chosen an early AP report to protect her name one last time—leave it to the scholars and other assholes to make that known].)

THE ROCK-AND-ROLL HANDBOOK

Chapter 1

Philosophy of Rock Stardom

All rock stars are different; all rock wannabes are the same. Remember this to avoid rock's most common pitfalls—greed, egomania, and self-delusion.

The difference between school and rock is that if you study rock you might actually learn something.

It's not the length, style, or even the presence of the hair that makes the rock star—it's the *attitude* of the hair.

Playing the guitar won't make you a rock star, but it gives you a better shot than playing the triangle, sousaphone, or ocarina.

You can wear cool clothes and have impressive tattoos and shocking piercings, but you'll be a bigger rock star if you can write a good song—you know?

All great rock songs are subversive in some way.

Your parents can do a lot of stuff for you, but you've got to become a rock star on your own.

When John Lennon wrote "Imagine," he was telling you about what being a rock star can mean even though you probably weren't born.

If you set your guitar on fire during a show and nobody cares, are you a rock star?

Once Alice Cooper outraged people; now he plays golf. The point is everybody becomes an old fart, even rock stars.

People who play in rock bands are different from you and me—they play in rock bands.

Groupies are God's answer to the question all rock stars face—who will I do after the show?

Drummer wisdom: One of the reasons rock stars go on tour is that if all the fans came to their house it would be too crowded.

There are ten songs every rock star should feel, heart and soul. What are yours?

Becoming a rock star is like winning the lottery—only with a soundtrack that you wrote.

When seventy-five thousand people sing along with you as you play a song you wrote, it's safe to assume you've made it as a rock star.

Rock star success is measurable: How many bands copy you? How many concerts sell out? How many assholes at your high school reunion act like long-lost friends?

Your career as a rock star is over when your most famous song is used to sell a car, jeans, or fast food no matter how much money you get.

THE ROCK-AND-ROLL HANDBOOK

Chapter 2

Career Wisdom and Advice

When you're working on a new set of rock song lyrics you should probably not be working on a rhyme for the words "cheese," "canasta," or "incontinence."

Three things you should do when you make it big as a rock star—buy your folks a mansion, buy your old school a music program, buy yourself a Porsche.

Rock stars lose their careers over one or more of these: Money, boy/girl friends, and substance abuse. Keep your mind on your music and your music on your mind.

If you want to make a good music video, ask yourself, "Would my high school buddies make fun of this?" about everything the director suggests that you do.

Rock star mantra: Get everything in writing. Get everything in writing. Get everything in writing. Get everything in writing. Get everything in writing. Get .
. .

In London they'll think you're just another pop star . . . you'll find that a relief after a while. . . .

The closer you get to the top of the music business, the less people will talk about music. Don't be fooled.

Despite our efforts to create a more tolerant society, it's better to be a skinny rock star than a fat one.

Never believe anything that the record company tells you (good or bad) about your voice/look/songwriting/musicianship.

If you think all the record company cares about is money, you're right.

There are three things that ruin a rock star's marriage: Tours, tours, and tours.

When Botox offers to sponsor your tour, you probably shouldn't be touring. . . .

The people that screwed you on your way to rock stardom will screw you on your way down—the people you screwed will try to get even.

Rock star mantra: Club owners are slime. Club owners are slime. Club owners are slime. Club owners are slime. Club owners are slime. Club owners are slime. . . .

When you're a rock star, you don't have to date supermodels—no, wait, what am I thinking. . . ?

When you find a guitar or microphone or amp or effects pedal or cymbal or any other tool of your trade that you love, buy several—trust me on this. . . .

The longer your career lasts, the less likely you are to see your work as important—this is good.

The shorter your career lasts, the more likely you are to see your work as misunderstood and unappreciated—this is bad.

Don't believe people who say your work stinks—don't believe people who say your work is the best ever. Believe yourself—you'll be fine.

THE ROCK-AND-ROLL HANDBOOK

Chapter 3

Fashion and Lifestyle

Rock star fashion tip: Wear denim and silk together unapologetically—you're a rock star!

Rock star mantra: Save some, spend a lot. Save some, spend a lot. Save some, spend a lot. Save some, spend a lot. Save some, spend a lot. . . .

Rock star fashion tip: Have a guitar to match every outfit . . . or is it the other way around. . . ?

Being a rock star means getting to have more fun with whipped cream than you ever dreamt possible.

If playing your instrument every day isn't something you feel compelled to do as if by magnetic force, you aren't a rock star.

Rock star and sports analogy: Groupies are like NFL quarterbacks—you can never have too many. . . .

Everyone gets lonely sometimes—but it's better being a lonely millionaire rock star than, say, a lonely dish washer in a greasy spoon. . . .

THE ROCK-AND-ROLL HANDBOOK

Chapter 4

Business Matters

Club owners like nothing better than to shortchange, or better yet, stiff bands. Bands cannot allow this. Hey, you're a rock star. You make sure of two things: You get paid and you get laid.

If a club owner refuses to pay the band, it is the band's responsibility to get compensation however they can. Any of the following work: Merchandise, trade, vandalism, blackballing.

Example: One band, call them Nothing Sacred, got shorted by a club owner who used them to fill his room, associated with his steak house, midweek for a so-called "college night."

The band was promised $450 for three hours' work. Owner only gave them $200. Claimed the 250 kids who bought $1200 worth of beer and burgers "didn't pay off."

The back exit to the room, used by bands to move equipment to/from the stage, went out by the storage hall where the huge cold storage unit full of steaks sat.

The band loaded its equipment—and $500 worth of steaks and prime rib.

When owner discovered his loss and threatened to sue band, band had a lawyer friend ask for receipts from night of show. That's how they knew about the

$1200 the s.o.b. made.

Nothing Sacred ate very, very well for a while. . .

.

THE ROCK-AND-ROLL HANDBOOK

Chapter 5

Infamous Last Words—Forewarned is Forearmed

"I'm just going to take my amp into the bathroom and practice that riff some more while I take a bath. . . ."

"We're only on the third floor—besides, if I jump out ten feet from the balcony, I'll land in the pool. . . ."

"It takes so long to gas up the van, man. I'm just going to light a smoke to kill time. . . ."

"I can drink that entire half-gallon of vodka in ten minutes and still play the show. . . ."

"What happens if you stick your tongue into a guitar jack while the amp's on . . . ?"

"Like hell I'll pay for this dope. I'm a rock star, man. What're you gonna do, kill me . . . ?"

"I'm just going to hang out with Sticks the drummer tonight. . . ."

THE ROCK-AND-ROLL HANDBOOK

Chapter 6

Rock Life's Great Questions

All *music* that makes parents uncomfortable is rock-and-roll and should be celebrated.

Rock stars may or may not have a shelf life. This is undetermined as of yet.

People who use the words "music industry"—as if "music" and "industry" should be referred to together—do harm to the world.

Rock-and-roll will never be dissociated from image, just as it will never be defined by image.

Beatlemania was from heaven; disco was from hell.

No amount of advertising use can damage a great rock song.

Beatles or Stones? Led Zeppelin or Steely Dan? REM or U2? Hmm . . .

Jesus, Mohammed, Lao Tse, and Siddhartha start a band. It's called . . . ? (Answers will vary.)

The opening chord of (ex. "A Hard Day's Night") expresses human potential. (Fill in with your own song.)

Strangers cannot be told about rock-and-roll.

The following are examples of unrecognized rock stars: Catullus, Chretien de Troyes, Christopher Marlowe, Benjamin Franklin, Goethe. Think of others . . .

Chapter 7

Drummers

Everyone in a band follows the drummer's beat—who the hell knows what the drummer follows.

Drummers take their shirts off more than any other band member. Only occasionally is it clear why.

Spinal Tap's spontaneously combusting drummers are based on actual incidents. You could look it up.

All drummers go to heaven. All lead singers go to hell. It is unclear why this is so.

In the 1960s a popular band had a drummer with a hook for a hand. No one thought this was odd.

Drummers are the most difficult members of bands to get and/or replace. No one knows why.

Actual quotes from drummers:
"Every day is like every other day except for its differences"; "What a hard day's night"; "I jumped into the river because someone said no one should."

THE ROCK-AND-ROLL HANDBOOK

Chapter 8

The Best Laid Plans . . .

Your band arrives for a show in HooHaw, West Virginia. There's no electricity. The promoter tells you, "The Snake Hollow Boys play without no electric. Y'all can, too."

Your band's van breaks down in the middle of the night in rural Kansas and the only car that comes by is Deputy Earl and his drug-sniffing Rottweiler, Ripper.

As the equipment is carried in by the roadies, your band hears a crash and Roadie Ray's voice says, "Damn—did we bring two bass drums?"

Your band arrives at their favorite all-night restaurant. You're met by a busload of stranded fundies on their way to a "Rock is Satanic" rally where your latest record is the text. . . .

Your band is about to appear in a showcase for record execs when your drummer looks at his hands and says, "Hey, look, I've got fins. . . ."

Your band's celebrating its first #1 at a chic place; you order six bottles of Dom Perignon and the wine steward brings out six Piper Heidsiecks instead. . . . No, wait . . .

Your band gets onto the local rock festival band roster; you go on at 7:45 A.M.

Glamour Boys: A *Rolling Stone* Interview
with Teddy Hatter and Jay Breeze

(Editor's Note: This interview with Teddy Hatter and
Jay Breeze of The Lost Generation was done in July
1977, just before the release of the album that critics
consider the best Lost Generation album, *Anthems for
Doomed Youth*. The group was about to embark on a
brief northeastern tour. That tour would be wildly
successful, selling out halls from Philly to Boston to
Buffalo. The interviewer, *RS* contributing editor
Charlie Beagle, i.e. me, a friend of Hatter and Breeze
since their college days at the University of North
Carolina, caught up with them in the late afternoon at
a midtown Manhattan restaurant where the "last
Romantics," as they're often called, waited for
bandmates Sid Vegas and Mick Norris to return from
a shopping spree. Both were nattily dressed, rock star
style—Hatter in a red satin blouse, tattered jeans,
and a black silk sport coat with red patch pockets,
Breeze in khaki jodhpurs, a purple T-shirt, a green
silk neckerchief, and a gray flannel coat in an
Edwardian cut that reached to mid-thigh. Both wore
boots [Breeze's looked like riding boots and had
rubberized soles] and sported their signature "longish
Beatle"- [circa *Revolver*] length hair, Hatter's dark
brown, Breeze's dirty blond. As the interview went on,
Jay [sort of] ate an actual meal. Teddy munched at a
club sandwich occasionally and smoked almost
nonstop. Drinks, especially brandy, flowed freely. . . .)

RS: You're rock stars as big as anyone these days,
guys. *How Do You Like Your Blue-Eyed Boys?* has sold
huge numbers, and your just-completed American

tour was entirely sold out, a first for the band. Feeling any pressure?

Teddy: (As he and Jay both laugh) About what? What to do with lots of money? Which fashion model to date? Whether to wear a silk or satin shirt with my jeans? How much to pay for that 1957 Fender Telecaster I've got my eye on? C'mon, Charlie, you can do better than that. . . .

RS: How about—for this album to be as successful as *Blue-Eyed Boys?*

Jay: Oh, that. (Laughs, then shakes his head) It's only math, man. Since *Blue-Eyed Boys?* sold twice as many as our first record, the new one only has to sell twice as many as the first two put together. At least that's what the record company thinks. So, no problems . . . By the way, we'll need you *to buy* your review copy, Charlie . . . (Winks).

Teddy: Besides, as long as Led Zeppelin is around, we're all playing for second place anyway. . . . So anything we do is just gravy for Atlantic. (*RS* note: Both Led Zeppelin and The Lost Generation record for Atlantic Records. The Lost Generation, as Led Zeppelin did earlier, record for Atlantic's Atco imprint. Zeppelin's Swan Song label is now distributed by Atlantic. . . .)

RS: Hmm. I'm hearing some professional jealousy. Do you guys know Zep? Anything personal between you?

Jay: We met them in England last year. We liked

them—I mean, Page is a little weird with that black magic shit, but Plant's really a pretty good guy—for a lead singer (Winks). Bonham's a drummer and acts like one (Everyone nods, acknowledging that drummers operate independent of most conventions—whether of time, space, or society). To me, the really interesting guy was Jones. He's a smart guy and a terrific musician. And they like our stuff and we like theirs, so it was all cool . . . you know. . . .

Teddy: Yeah, if they just didn't sell so many more records than us, we'd all be blood brothers. . . . (Laughter all around) Hey, isn't this interview supposed to be about us? Zeppelin gets enough ink in this rag. . . .

RS: Okay. Well how about this, then? Some critics, despite the band's success, have complained that Lost Generation is nothing but a throwback to the British pop bands of the sixties—you write clever love songs and dress interestingly and you're good-looking. You're basically a teeny-bopper band. . . .

Teddy: Well, first, critics—all those at this magazine as well as you, Lester Bangs (He points in the general direction of outside)—suck. Second . . . well, there is no second. Critics suck. . . .

Jay: Teddy may be right, but there might be a reason for the knee-jerk reaction we've had in some quarters. No one else has really followed The Beatles' path—we've tried. And that's not a wrong path, Charlie—we concentrate on writing melodic rock songs and presenting them with some verve to push the "Beatle model" beyond where they left off—around the time of *Revolver*. . . . As for our being good-looking and dressing—interestingly (Makes a face), aren't those *ad hominem* attacks . . . ?

RS: Lennon himself said, "I don't believe in Beatles," Jay. . . .

Jay: When Lennon says that—he's not really saying that The Beatles were bad or that they didn't matter. He's saying that he's not interested in being a Beatle anymore—it may happen that one or all of us decide we don't want to be The Lost Generation at some point in the future. That doesn't mean we think what we did was bad—just that we've moved beyond it and want to do something else.

(*RS* note: At this revelation by his friend and songwriting partner, Teddy Hatter looks stunned. It seems that the idea that his band will end its career at some point has never occurred to him.)

RS: Let's get to some history.

Teddy: Well, you've written about how you left the band and Jay joined, Charlie. And you've also written about how we ended up with Sid as our drummer. So what part of our history do you want us to talk about?

RS: Tell us how you got your record deal.

Teddy: Jay?

Jay: (Starting to eat a bowl of soup he's just been

brought) Your show . . .

Teddy: Well, it's one of those "one in a million" things, like the manuscript pulled from a publisher's slush pile that becomes a bestseller. We were making pretty decent money by then. We were playing shows at rock clubs like The Blue Max in Greensboro, Town Hall in Chapel Hill, and The Double Door in Charlotte (*RS* note: all clubs in North Carolina). We were playing lots of shows at colleges—mostly frat parties and stuff—doing a mix of covers and our own tunes. Oddly enough, it was at a frat party at Duke where we got our break. The daughter of a guy whose accounting firm serviced Atlantic Records came to the party, heard us, and liked us. She then came to see us at Town Hall where we played a show of mostly our own stuff. She approached us after the show and asked us if we had a record or tape because she wanted to make her dad listen and pass it along to the record execs at Atlantic. We gave her a cassette of some stuff we'd recorded at a studio in Greensboro through our agent. The quality wasn't as good as you'd expect because the studio was owned by a guy named Chuck Nightingale who has an orchestra that plays society dances and stuff like that. He wouldn't let us bring in our own producer—we had to use his guy, who was probably sixty years old and recorded us as if we were a thirty-piece orchestra. We set up the equipment in the middle of a big room with microphones all around us and they just kind of turned on the tape. But it was all we had, so we gave it to her. She took it and disappeared. That was . . . December of '73. We didn't hear anything for a month, so we wrote it off as "cute chick talks us out of a free cassette."

Jay: (Looking up from his soup and smiling slyly) Teddy was such a serious student he forgot about the end of the semester and the holiday break. . . .

Teddy: (Looking at Jay) Suck my doo-doo. . . .

Jay: Don't get romantic. . . .

RS: The story?

Jay: Sheila, the fan from Duke, had gone home for the holidays and was nagging her dad to share the tape with somebody in A&R at Atlantic. Then she went with her dad and mom to a holiday party Atlantic threw and gave the tape (Unbeknownst to her dad) to Ahmet Ertegun. . . . And he promised her he'd listen to it. . . .

Teddy: Yeah. We heard that story much later, of course. Well, sometime about four or five weeks later, about mid-January of 1974, we were sitting around the fireplace in the Kimesville lake house we were living in, listening to—I think it was Elton John—we were really into *Tumbleweed Connection*—Jay?

Jay: (While flirting with some women at a nearby table) That sounds right. . . .

Teddy: So we're chilling by the fire—it was early. . . .

Jay: (Laughing) Yeah, about ten, ten-thirty, eleven in the morning . . . really early for musicians. . . .

Teddy: . . . and the phone rang. Jay and I argued over

who should answer it.

Jay: (Sending an omelet back to the kitchen because it is "too oozy") *I* won.

Teddy: Anyway, *I* answered the phone. And it was Jerry Wexler's secretary. She wanted to know when we could come to NYC to do a session. . . .

Jay: Actually, to record some demos, she said. . . .

Teddy: (Exasperated) You want to tell this?

(Jay holds up both hands in an *I'm out of this* gesture)

Teddy: (Smiling at Jay) They wanted us to come to NYC to do a session and record some demos—(He turns, but Jay is being served another omelet and waves him off)—so we set up a time about two weeks later . . . ? (He looks at Jay again, but Jay, mouth full of omelet, merely nods and waves him off again) So anyway, we called our booking agent and found out we had to play a show in Columbia, SC, the night before the session . . . so Jay called Wexler's office back and . . . (He leans back and waits. Jay looks up from his omelet. Teddy gestures for him to continue.)

Jay: (Stopping his eating to light a cigarette) Well, we were jumping up and down and hugging each other and doing all the other silly shit you'd expect from a couple of guys who've just been asked to come to New York and make a record. . . .

Teddy: Demo . . .

Jay: (Rolling his eyes at Teddy) A *demo* record would do. Then it occurred to me that we should get with Paul Sorrento, our booking agent, and get the schedule opened up so we could go to New York. So I called him. That's when we found out about the Columbia show. Just then Mick and Sid came in. They'd been out getting coffee and doughnuts. Sid suggested we get Paul to put another band in for the show at USC (*RS* note: that's the University of South Carolina, not Southern California.) But Mick and Teddy both said no, we needed the money for the New York trip. . . .

Teddy: So Jay just went to the phone and called Jerry Wexler's office. The secretary had stepped out and Jerry Wexler himself answered the phone. And cool as a cucumber Jay explained about the problem and our need to play the Columbia show for the money. . . .

Jay: And Jerry Wexler says, "What time does the show end?" I say, "We usually have to stop playing at midnight." Then Jerry says, "How long does it take to get to the airport?" I said, "I'm not sure. Maybe fifteen minutes?"

Teddy: So Jerry says, "There'll be a private jet to pick you up at the airport in Columbia. Takeoff will be at 12:30. If you're there, you fly here, we sign contracts, and you begin recording your first album the next evening. If you aren't, we forget the whole thing." And Jay, ever the cautious one, says, "We can't make that timetable, Mr. Wexler. We have to pack our gear after the show. We can't leave our amps and sound system. What if you don't want us once we get there?"

RS: Damn, Jay. You've got one of the gurus of the record industry telling you you're as good as signed and you're worrying about amps and PA equipment?

Jay: We had a lot of money tied up in our gear.

(Everyone laughs. Jay blushes slightly. A well-known fashion model comes into the restaurant. As she makes her way among the tables, she spots Jay and Teddy and blows them kisses. They look at each other, each seeming to say, "That for you?" then both blow her kisses. She laughs and tosses her blonde mane, then takes a seat at a table with a man well into his forties who frowns in the direction of our table. Both Jay and Teddy make gestures to him reminiscent of those one might see from The Three Stooges.)

RS: Does *that* happen often?

Teddy: Every day.

(He and Jay try not to look at each other, but once they do they break into laughter again. Jay calls over a waiter and orders brandy and soda all around. Once the drinks are served, we get back to the story.)

RS: So finish the story, one of you.

Teddy: I'll let Jay finish.

Jay: You sure?

Teddy: You created this part of the legend, man. You tell it.

Jay: (Smiling) Okay, then. So I tell Jerry Wexler about the gear and he's quiet for what seems like a long time. I even begin to think he's going to tell me just to forget it. I can literally feel sweat beading on my upper lip. Finally Jerry says, "Don't you have roadies?" And I say, "Well, Scott and Van help us out sometimes." He says, "Have them help you out this time. Let them pack the road gear and drive it home for you. You guys just bring your guitars and suitcases. Tell your drummer we'll set him up with a kit here." So I say, "Yes sir." And he says, "Well, I've got a session to go to. We'll talk when you get up here." So I said thanks and goodbye and was starting to hang up when Jerry stopped me by yelling, "Hey!" I respond and he says, "Just one thing more." I say, "Sir?" And he says, "Get to the plane when you can. It'll wait for you."

RS: What'd you say?

Jay: (Laughing) I said, "Yes sir!"

RS: So you went to New York and began recording?

Teddy: Yeah, pretty much. As we found out later, Ertegun dug the cassette, played it for Wexler, and they both agreed that they wanted to sign us and get a record underway as soon as possible. Turns out they'd both liked Badfinger and wanted a band in that vein, American if possible, for their stable. They'd considered The Raspberries but didn't think they could get them away from Epic.

RS: The Raspberries? And why an American band?

Jay: You've heard *Overnight Sensation*. The Raspberries might have worked out well for them. And they wanted an American band because Ahmet always regretted the way Buffalo Springfield fell apart. He'd felt they could have been an American equivalent to the biggest English bands—maybe not The Beatles, but The Stones or The Who. . . .

RS: Hmm . . . Let me change the focus here. Tell me about the new album. First, the title—*Anthems for Doomed Youth* . . .

Teddy: That's just Jay again. He usually names our albums. . . . We all like the literary allusions, though.

RS: This one's from Wilfred Owen, right? The World War I poet . . . That's a pretty serious poem. Is this a serious album?

Teddy: They're all serious albums, Charlie . . . (Snorts and laughs).

Jay: This album has some stuff on it that I like to think is pushing forward for us. "The Rock-and-Roll Ideal" and "Loss of Control" are more philosophical than our usual stuff. . . .

Teddy: And "Renascence" and "Normal but Helpless" and "Can't Be Helped"—yeah, this is a pretty serious record compared to *Blue-Eyed Boys?* We were trying to do something more on this album. *Blue-Eyed Boys?* let us go about as far as we could with our love songs concept. We wanted to expand the subject matter . . . Jay?

Jay: We had some of these songs already done, but they didn't fit the character of the first two albums. We've had "Rock-and-Roll Ideal" and "Renascence" since maybe 1973. . . .

Teddy: And it was Mick who said, "We've got these songs that move us forward. Let's put an album together that takes the next step." Sid encouraged us, too. So we went to work and wrote "Loss of Control" and "Can't Be Helped." Then Sid made a comment while we were on tour. . . .

RS: Uh oh. I sense a drummer story coming.

Teddy: (Laughing) Yeah, we were stuck in an airport in Kansas City or somewhere. . . .

Jay: It was Lincoln, Nebraska, I think. . . .

Teddy: Okay, Lincoln, and it was foggy, then it got cold, then it started to snow . . . we were sitting around this airport and it was like two in the morning and it was clear we weren't going to get out that night. And Paul couldn't find us hotel rooms for some reason. . . .

Jay: (Lighting another cigarette) That might have been because it was the night after the big Nebraska/Oklahoma football game. . . .

Teddy: So we're sitting in those molded chairs in a waiting area and Paul shows up again and tells us that he still hasn't found rooms but Scott's talking to some airport people who are trying some other places nearby, and Paul asks, "How we doing, guys?" It's his standard question that we've heard a million times. Anyway, the rest of us mumbled obscenities of one sort or another, but Sid looked at Paul and said, "Feeling pretty much the usual, Paul. Normal but helpless. . . ." Jay and I looked at each other in the same instant and I reached for my guitar and by the time Scott showed up about thirty minutes later with news that he'd found us rooms at a downtown hotel, we'd knocked out the major part of the song.

RS: So what's next for The Lost Generation?

(Both Jay and Teddy break into laughter)

Teddy: Oh, I don't know—a tour, maybe?

Jay: Actually it's a bit better than the usual. After a few dates here in the northeast, we're off to Europe for three weeks. We go to Oslo first, then to Copenhagen, then to Stockholm, then south to Lisbon. . . .

RS: So, will you go to Germany?

Jay: (Narrowing his eyes) Are you asking if I'll get to see my son?

(RS note: Breeze has recently learned that he has a son from a brief relationship with a German art student he met during the band's 1976 European tour. Though they have no plans to marry, Breeze has officially accepted parental responsibility and set up a trust fund for the child.)

RS: Yeah, I guess I am.

(*RS* note: Hatter and Breeze pass a look that suggests the interviewer has changed from their longtime friend to a scandal-sheet reporter.)

Teddy: So it's going to go this way now, Charlie?

RS: Look, I'm going to ask about things I want to know and I think *RS* readers want to know about. . . .

Teddy: Yeah, well, I'd expect this shit from some of the rags we deal with, but . . .

Jay: (Who has been musing) It's a fair question, Teddy. (He sits quiet for a moment, then begins softly) I met Marlene at an art exhibition in Frankfurt. I was just killing time on an off day. To start up a conversation with this striking blonde, I admired a piece of sculpture and it turned out she was the artist. She's both a working artist and working on a doctorate in art history. She's a smart, beautiful woman—and a Lost Generation fan . . . (We all smile, a little uneasily) and we just sort of took off like a rocket. She traveled with us through the next month and a half all over Europe, then she had to get back to Frankfurt for school or work or . . . hell, I don't know why love affairs end—do you?

RS: So you just thought of it as a tour romance . . . ?

(Jay lights a cigarette and takes a long drink of brandy and soda. He tinkles the ice in the glass to get a waiter's attention and orders another round for all of us. It seems he may have nothing else to say at this time.)

Teddy: (His voice testy) Got enough for *RS* readers yet, Charlie?

Jay: Lay off Charlie, Teddy. Charlie's a journalist and he's our friend. Imagine having this conversation with one of those bottom feeders in London. . . .

(Teddy Hatter grunts and takes a brandy and soda from the waiter and gulps at it. We all drink from our brandies. Time passes. Jay puts down his glass and takes another long drag from a cigarette. . . .)

Jay: So about six months later I get a letter from Marlene. I'd called her a couple of times and written to her, too. No response. So I let it go. Then I get this letter and she tells me she's pregnant. . . .

RS: How'd that feel?

Jay: (Smiling wistfully) Just about like you'd think. I called her right away and we talked for almost three hours. She didn't want anything for herself. She just asked if I wanted to help with the baby. She also told me she didn't respond earlier because she thought she couldn't keep the pregnancy from me and she was afraid I'd try to get her to abort and she couldn't bear the thought of doing so because our affair meant that much to her—but she didn't see us as a couple, so . . .

RS: (Interrupting) I think that's all *RS* readers want to know, Jay.

(There is silence for several moments, all three of us looking at our glasses between drinks from them. Then Jay smiles at the interviewer and he smiles back. Both look at Teddy and he finally breaks into a grin.)

Teddy: Anything you want to ask *me* about, Charlie?

RS: Damaged any hotel rooms, lately, Teddy?

(Laughter all around—Lost Generation is legendary for "hotel havoc," as they call their penchant for easing the boredom of touring with wild parties that usually result in heavy hotel-damage fees. At this point Mick Norris and Sid Vegas come in from shopping and the interview dissolves in greetings, even more drink orders, and eventually [thanks to all the booze] maudlin reminiscing. . . .)

UNC Student Killed in Single-Car Accident

Chapel Hill (AP) — A 22-year-old female, a senior at UNC Chapel Hill, was killed in a one-car accident early this morning while returning to campus from an off-campus party. Details are scant at present, but it appears that both rain and alcohol were factors in the accident. The identity of the student has not been revealed pending notification of next of kin.

NC Highway Patrol Spokesman Chuck Wills stated: "The death of this beautiful young person at the start of her life in such a tragic manner points again to the need for everyone to be vigilant in preventing friends from driving if they have been consuming alcohol. The NC Highway Patrol urges all citizens to act responsibly both in their own driving behavior and in their dealings with friends who may be tempted to drink and drive."

From *The Reidsville Review*, Feb. 9, 1993:

[*Reidsville Review*] Editor's Note: As part of *The Review*'s "We Remember Jay" coverage of the death of Reidsville native, rock star Jay Breeze (Jay Brent), we offer these remarks by his friend and bandmate Mick Norris (Michael Grover Blaine Norris III) taken from Mr. Norris's eulogy at Jay's memorial service, which he kindly edited into an essay of sorts and allows us to publish below:

SOME WORDS ABOUT JAY
By Mick Norris

Hi, Everyone:

My name is Mick Norris. Actually, it's Michael Grover Blaine Norris III. That's the name my mom and dad gave me back in 1952 when I was born. My mom still calls me Michael. My dad still calls me Mike. In school I was Mike.

I've always hated the name Mike. Even though my friends called me Mike and my dad called me Mike and my first girlfriend, whom I still love, I think, and who's here today (aside: hi, Lea) still calls me Mike—though she asks me, "Should I call you Mick? Or can I still call you Mike?" whenever I see her (aside: call me whatever, babe)—I still hate the name Mike.

Now I'm Mick. And I'm Mick thanks to Jay Breeze—whose real name is John Jay Brent. Jay decided he wanted a stage name and took the surname Breeze—just like that.

(I know there's a verb/tense thing—present instead of past—going on above but I'll get to that later.)

So over a beer one night after a show I asked him about it. The name change, I mean. And he said, "I like the name Breeze. So I've named myself Breeze. Rock-and-roll is about doing what you like, Mike."

That knocked me out.

So I thought about it a while and then I remembered something. When I was thirteen back in 1965, I was at White Lake, NC, with my parents for a weekend. I spent a dollar at the White Lake arcade and played "Satisfaction" by The Rolling Stones ten times in a row. Drove everyone out of the place. I just liked the way it sounded. And I liked the singer's name—Mick Jagger. And I looked up some info on Mick and found out his real name is Michael.

So I became Mick Norris. And I really like being Mick Norris.

I owe my happiness in being Mick Norris to Jay Breeze.

(I still haven't gotten to the verb tense issue above, but I need to talk about something else first, so it'll have to wait.)

Bands are strange entities. They're amalgams and yet they're like single-cell organisms. You have to have distinct, identifiable personalities as members to appeal to as wide a range of—Tastes? Interests? Libidos?—as possible, but these personalities have to merge into a single—voice, I guess is the best term. It has to be easy for people to go, "Hey, that's—" and turn up their radios.

The Lost Generation has the best of both—we

have Teddy the mysterious, Captain Nemo as guitar hero; Sid, glib and wacky, Mr. Macawber as drummer; me, witty, good-looking (!), reckless, Don Juan on rhythm guitar; and Jay—beautiful, haunted Jay—Romeo as bassist. But you hear a Lost Generation song—"Leaves Like Love on Fire," "Mary, Quite Contrary," "The Rock-and-Roll Ideal"—and you know immediately it's us—one voice.

One for all, all for one. The Musketeers had it right. So *did* we.

And I've finally used the past tense. About both the band and Jay by extension. You have no idea what doing that takes out of me.

I guess it's time to say to Jay what I always used to say at the end of a tour: "Love you, bro. How about you have another great tune when I see you again?"

Thanks for listening (or reading), everyone.

(Editor's Final Note, written in desperation after a scotch or three too many: What follows is a fragment of a piece I did on Jay Breeze for *Rolling Stone* that was supposed to appear in the January 7, 1979 issue of the magazine. Anyway, too late for anything but history, here is as much as I wrote. *Après celui-ci, le déluge.* . . . C.B.)

Romeo in New York: Jay Breeze of The Lost Generation Bites the Big Apple on its Neck and Leaves a Hickey

Going around with rock stars is always a pain in the ass, but part of my job since I write about them for a living. They never show up anywhere on time, they cause trouble everywhere they go, and they never carry money, so you can get stuck with some hellacious checks.

Going around with your friends is usually great. Friends (well, most of them) show up when they're supposed to, try to keep you (and themselves) out of trouble, and always help with the check.

So what happens when you go around with one of your friends and he's a rock star?

That's what I wanted to know. So I talked my bosses at *Rolling Stone* into letting me go around with Jay Breeze, a friend of mine since high school days who also happens to be the bassist (and, for all intents, lead singer) of one of the most successful bands in America, The Lost Generation. The band's latest release, *War and Peace and Boredom*, is surging up the charts and Jay is in NYC to appear on Tom Snyder's program *Tomorrow* (among other things) along with bandmate Teddy Hatter (another old friend—full disclosure: In another life, I was a member of the band that became The Lost Generation, a fact about which I've written before for this magazine. In fact, Jay Breeze replaced me—with my blessing—in the group). I spent November 22–26 of 1978 in New York going around with my friend Jay (and much of the time with Teddy, too), whose behavior seemed so far from the norm of rock star assholery as to make us both a little uncomfortable.

Andy Warhol's Factory is a shithole of a place. It used to be at Union Square but now it's here on Broadway. This is my second trip. (I came here to some sort of thing that Warhol was having for John and Yoko. This was early, during what we now call John's "hermit" period, and I just wanted to catch him for a moment to get a good quote for *RS*. He didn't show, but Elton John and Dylan did, and I got a quote from Bob that I used—but you don't want to know this crap. . . .) I really hate the place—it's largely a parade of assholes too snooty to talk to you until they hear your name and realize you're famous (or you're like me and write about the famous) and the occasional freak (tranny, porn actor/actress, etc.) who wanders by (though the latter types are much rarer at The Factory these days because Andy's tightened security so much since the Solanas woman shot him). It's not a comfortable place—there just aren't good places to sit, and you're forever in someone's way.

I'm here with Jay (and Teddy Hatter, his co-composer in The Lost Generation). Warhol has asked them to write a song for a new film he's doing. This seems like a bad practical joke to me—Warhol could get Lou Reed or John Cage to score music for him and they're a hell of a lot more *simpatico* with his artistic vision than Jay and Teddy will ever be. But what do I know?

There are a number of very attractive women here today for some reason, and they've discovered that a couple of rock stars are waiting to see Warhol (who's ignoring the guys, it seems to me—he set up this appointment and he's already nearly ninety minutes late from the time he set "so no one has to wait"—of course, the guys were forty-five minutes late getting here themselves, so we're just getting square, I suppose). The beauties cruise by where we're waiting (I guess it's a reception area, but it's unlike any I've ever seen—it's about as receptive as a warehouse vestibule) in ones and twos and smile at Jay and Teddy who either look at them as dispassionately as if they were mannequins, or don't look at them at all. They have rock star behavior down pat. I, on the other hand, smile pleasantly at each of these lovelies, but they give me pretty much the same look they're getting from Jay and Teddy.

I should have stayed in the damned band.

Finally, there's a bustle down one of the hallways leading off this entrance and Warhol arrives, platinum wig and all, with a retinue of half a dozen assistants. He apologizes to the boys for making them wait, Jay and Teddy apologize for being late in the first place, and we're good to go, it seems. Just as we turn to go to his office to chat he turns to me. "Why did you make fun of my wig, Charlie Beagle?" he asks.

"Didn't know I did, Andy," I say, overstepping, calling him by his first name, to let him know I don't much give a shit whether he likes something I wrote or not. Trust me, it's the only way with these people— you know, the famous. . . .

"Well," he says, winking coyly, "I liked it. So many people have mentioned it to me. I love the publicity."

And with that he links his arm in mine and we're walking down the hallway to his office, Jay and Teddy in tow. I look back at them and shrug. They just grin and blow kisses at the pretty girls who seem to have

153

lined the hallway and are ogling them. Finally one of the beauties flashes her breasts at us—then suddenly all the girls are getting topless and we're walking a parade route of hooters at attention.

It's a set-up, of course. Warhol loves this kind of stuff. I glance around and his assistants are concentrating on looking really innocent. It's then that I realize Warhol is as much the object of this ruse as Jay and Teddy.

Jay and Teddy's rock star indifference breaks a little here and they ogle these bare-chested beauties as any healthy young men would, whispering and laughing between themselves. Warhol's assistants seem delighted. Breaking people down to their ids seems a preoccupation of The Factory crowd.

I must admit, though, that there are some fine mammaries on display.

Warhol releases my arm and raises his omnipresent Minox camera. "I really should get pictures of this," he says, and begins snapping away at Jay and Teddy, the girls nothing more than a lascivious backdrop. It's art imitating life imitating art. . . .

We're being whisked away in a limo that picked us up at Warhol's Factory (ah, rock star travel) to Ralph Lauren's digs in midtown Manhattan.

Jay's meeting with Ralph Lauren is as unlike the meeting with Andy Warhol as accidentally smoking opium is to sipping Piper Heidsieck on purpose.

(Teddy's off meeting one of the other gods of fashion, NYC-style, Calvin Klein, and I'm guessing getting similar treatment.)

Lauren, the fastest-rising fashion designer in

America, is looking to dress a rock star. He's settled on Jay Breeze. Ralph seems to think his whole "country gentry" design vision suits Jay perfectly. The problem is, Jay created his own style with the jodhpurs and silk kerchiefs and long jackets. Kids copy *his style*. Now Lauren wants to appropriate Jay and make him a mannequin for *Ralph Lauren style*—and there's only one reason for that—$$$ for Ralph Lauren. . . .

Okay, time for an aside.

I think this letting designers dress musicians is bullshit, but no one's asked my opinion. The more music ties itself to fashion, the more likely it is to *become* fashion—and that way lies madness—and eventual irrelevancy.

What really makes me uneasy is that Jay and Teddy are so nonchalant about this stuff. "Do you really think getting free clothes for a few magazine shoots and wearing them onstage occasionally is really evil, Charlie?" Jay asks me in the limo on the way to Lauren's place. Teddy and I have been going at it hammer and tongs since we left Warhol's studio. The guys have agreed to write a song about "the mystery of love" (as Warhol put it) for a new film Warhol is working on, called, tentatively, "America in Love." I had started in on the two of them as an assistant walked us back to the reception area from Warhol's office where our driver stood waiting somewhat dumbfounded by the stream of beautiful girls filing out of the building.

"So, it's 'compose on commission,' now?" I say.

"Dammit, Charlie, what the hell's wrong with you?" Teddy growls. "If Warhol wants to us to write a song for *his* movie, how's that different from some

Hollywood guy asking us to write a song for some Hollywood flick?"

"It's not," I reply.

Jay knows full well I'm lying in wait for Teddy, so he intercedes. "Charlie thinks we're selling out, Teddy. That's why he's on our case."

Teddy is apoplectic. "Charlie, the object of all this is to make all the fucking money we can. Hell, The Beatles did movie music. And Elvis made dozens of movies—"

"Yeah, and Elvis wasn't worth a shit once he went into movies," I growl. "And as for The Fabs, Paul and George did scores on their own. They didn't violate the integrity of the band—"

"Christ, Charlie," Jay begins. Then he stops and looks out the window.

I've dealt with this before. Jay Breeze is not a guy to let his emotions out. He'll reel himself in and reset whatever button I've pushed before he speaks again.

By this time we've reached Calvin Klein's. The driver pulls up and a Klein assistant opens the car door for Teddy. He looks at Jay, then me, and says, "Charlie, be good to Jay or I'll kick your ass." Then he's gone. I note the pop of flashes as paparazzi snap pictures of the rock star entering the fashion star's lair. It's not unlike the snap of Warhol's Minox multiplied. Life and art commingling again, I guess. . .
.

Well, now we're back to Jay's question: "Do you really think getting free clothes for doing a few magazine shoots and wearing them onstage occasionally is really evil, Charlie?" he's asked me as we make our way the few blocks between Calvin Klein's place and Ralph Lauren's.

I'm formulating an answer as we pull up at Ralph Lauren's shop. A guy who looks like he's ready to go grouse shooting in Manhattan opens the limo door and Jay steps out, me on his heels.

There are paparazzi here, too, and they begin shooting as soon as Jay has cleared the car. Jay freezes as he always does—he hates them but he doesn't have the heart to confront them or ruin their pictures.

But I'm there and I have no such foibles. I step in front of Jay and begin flipping the bird in every direction. The Lauren assistant is startled, but he quickly begins aping my behavior. The photogs are soon shouting obscenities at us, but the flashes stop and we make it into Lauren's place with no more pics.

(Editor's Note: Sure, the rags would publish pics of us flipping the bird nowadays, but back in 1978 that wasn't the case. So my ploy worked okay. C.B.)

Once inside, Jay turns to me and says, "Thanks, Charlie. I hate those guys, but I can't . . ."

"I love it, Jay. You know that. And I can't wait until one of them shows pics to Jann or Ben and they realize that I'm the guy ruining the pics."

We're both laughing as an attractive young woman who looks like she's going to lunch at someone's country estate comes up to us with a trayful of champagne flutes. "This is Piper Heidsieck, 1975, an outstanding year," we're told.

A quick count tells me there are eight flutes on the tray. I look at Jay. "You get eight?" he asks. I nod.

"Stand right there," he tells the woman with the tray. She does.

In short order he and I polish off four flutes apiece. "Got any more?" I ask.

The poor woman looks at us, her expression somewhere between astonishment and fear, and mumbles, "I'll see." Then she's moving away as quickly as she can without breaking all those nice crystal flutes.

Jay and I look at each other a moment, then burst out laughing. No matter how much clothing Ralph Lauren gives my friend, I know he's going to keep right on being a rock star.

I should do a longer section on the time with Ralph Lauren, but I can't think of anything nasty to say. Lauren is a charming guy, as gentlemanly as you'd want him to be, and his assistants actually assisted us rather than hovered slightly menacingly like those flying monkeys over at Warhol's place. Jay and I went through a couple more bottles of that superb Piper Heidsieck (drinking considerably more slowly so as to appreciate the flavor and not cause the assistant serving us any more heart palpitations). Jay tried on several outfits, all of which looked good (Jay, though, has that rock star aura thing going so it's hard to determine how much Lauren's clothes were doing for him and how much he was doing for Lauren's clothes).

Lauren's ideas for Jay are logical extensions of how Jay dresses and how his dress could be re-envisioned by the country squire of Manhattan. He starts with a pair of jodhpurs then moves into jeans and finally into some khakis. The pants are paired with T-shirts and Western-style shirts (those things with the snaps for buttons, which I could tell Jay hated. Lauren senses it, too, and offers an alternative—a tunic-looking thing like those shirts John Wayne used to wear that buttons on both sides. Jay digs those.) There's more stuff, but this ain't *Vogue* I'm writing for.

The best moment comes when Jay asks me for an opinion. He's wearing a pair of khakis with side pockets like military pants, a cream-colored shirt, a gold neckerchief and what R.L. calls a sack coat in a blue color so dark it looks black at times as Jay walks about in it.

"How do you like this, Charlie?" He stands before me and holds his arms out at his sides then turns this way and that to model the coat.

And, God help me, I'm reduced to paraphrasing Daisy Buchanan: "It almost makes me sad—I've never seen such a—beautiful outfit, Jay," I stammer.

Lauren just stands by beaming at both of us.

Tavern on the Green's Crystal Room is not a good choice for dinner if you're famous. I've never understood Jay Breeze's fascination with it. Because he's a rock star, they always put him next to the windows (fame hath its privileges).

This is where the story stops being "typical celebrity shit" and starts being The Madness of King Jay, Romeo in New York, and the chaos theory of rock-stardom lab test. . . .

That's all there is. Sorry. I know, but what can I say?

I was at work on this right after I did the visit to

NYC in November of 1978 that provided the material for this piece. One of my "friends" called me and said we needed to meet for a drink. I met him, we had several drinks, and he then confessed to shtupping my fiancée. Then, because he was my "friend," he told me about two other guys, both good "friends," that she was also sleeping with. And started me on that downward spiral I spent months swirling in before I finally got my feet under me again. . . .

I took a couple of stabs at trying to write the profile but I was too fucked up emotionally and chemically to get it done—and when I finally got straightened out enough to do the piece a few months later, Jann (or Ben, I forget which) was no longer interested in profiling Jay. Plus, both were pissed at me for having gone off the reservation for about six months. So Jay got screwed out of what would have been a nice piece about him. Both Ahmet and Jerry were pissed, too, since the publicity would have helped sales of their album War and Peace and Boredom. *It took me a frickin' year to get everybody back on board with me. I guess I owe Hunter some thanks for that, but to hell with him.*

I just can't finish it. I've tried—especially in these last months while working at piecing together this book.

I've wanted to.

Desperately.

For Jay. Because I love him.

But it just won't come to me. I sit and stare at my notes and read over them again and again. And wish everything was different from how it is.

Yeah, this leaves you hanging, wanting more, feeling cheated, wishing you knew the rest. So do I.

I feel that way about Jay's life and work—as I bet you do.

Reader, alias, twin . . .

The Lost Generation: Selected Song Lyrics

(Editor's Note: What I've done here is exactly what I said above—I've chosen a song from each of the albums, one that I like—sometimes for my own esoteric reasons. You might have chosen others. That's you. I'm me . . . C.B.)

(All songs by Jay Breeze and Teddy Hatter)

From *We Are All The Lost Generation*:

"Boys With Guitars and Dreams"

You see them in the music stores
You see them in clubs,
And you see them in shopping malls;
They're always working on their style
Yeah, they're working on their smiles,
And they're working on the way that they walk;
They've got a lot of crazy schemes
And they seem to find ways,
Though they don't always find the means;
They act a little stupid sometimes—
They're just practicing reacting,
Practicing reacting to screams . . .
They're boys with guitars and dreams. . . .

Their parents teach them right from wrong
And they teach them little songs
Then they send them away to school;
But there it's "Everyone is the same!"

So they learn to play games
And they learn to obey lots of rules—
Pretty soon they know the routine
They know to fit in—they wonder
If life's what it seems—
'Til one day when they hear that loud noise
And they know it's for them
And they think they've found out what life means . . .
For boys with guitars and dreams. . . .

Watch them struggle; watch them make it,
Sometimes watch them fly . . .

See them stumble; see them fall down,
Sometimes, see them die. . . .

I saw him in a shopping mall—
He was stealing *Sgt. Pepper*,
He was hoping he wouldn't get caught;
I saw him in a music store—
He was fingering a Fender
Like it was a .44;
I saw him in a club downtown—
He was playing really loud
He was hoping someone listened at all;
Sometimes I feel so sorry for them
'Cause I know that they're all,
I know that they're all like me . . .
They're boys with guitars and dreams. . . .

From *How Do You Like Your Blue-Eyed Boys?*:

"River Kisses"

Down by the river,
Right off the boat-landing road;
Late summer nights
We met those girls (we met those girls) . . .

No one in love there—
We were just sowing some oats
Having some fun
So were those girls (so were those girls) . . .

That summer long gone
I drove by there just last week—
And all at once
Lived it again (lived it again) . . .

Like I was right there
Right in that moment again;
What brought it on?
I can't recall (I can't recall) . . .

There were
River kisses . . .
River kisses . . .
And so much more, I can't recall. . . .

Life . . . is a river—
It has shoals,
It has falls . . .

Time—is a river

Through our lives
It flows on. . . .

Memories haunt us
We never know when they'll come
Sometimes through sight
Sometimes through touch (sometimes through touch)

They drive us crazy;
Why won't they let us move on?
Give us some peace,
Leave us alone (leave us alone). . . .

All those
River kisses . . .
River kisses . . .
And so much more, I can't recall. . . .

From *Anthems for Doomed Youth*:

"Leaves Like Love on Fire"

I'm walking in the park
Where we talked of this—
Talked of that—and where we first kissed;
All the leaves on fire . . .

Another autumn now
And I think about
What we did—and how we put out
Love like leaves on fire. . . .

Maybe it wasn't you
And it wasn't I
Maybe some loves just die—
Like the leaves

Coming October dark
And I should go home
Shouldn't think of what we did wrong. . . .

Maybe it wasn't you
And it wasn't I
Maybe some loves just die—
Like the leaves

Yet I keep standing here
As my heart still grieves
Grieves and burns—like these autumn leaves
Leaves like love on fire. . . .

From *War and Peace and Boredom*:

"Like Russian Winter"

A May afternoon:
There is nothing more for us to say—
We both know you must go . . .
You drive away
And though warm spring sunlight filters down—
To me it feels like snow . . .

And when you were gone,
It felt like Russian winter;
Everything gone cold and dark—
And I stood there helpless,
Like the Tolstoy hero
Waiting for the bomb to drop. . . .

An August evening
I am talking with a mutual friend—
I sense there's something that she doesn't want to say
. . .
She finally tells me
That you have found someone to take my place—
Then everything goes gray . . .

And when she was gone,
It felt like Russian winter;
Everything gone cold and dark—
So I stood there helpless,
Like the Tolstoy hero
Waiting for the bomb to drop. . . .

A November night

I am dreaming of you once again—
We are somewhere—it is cold . . .
You call my name
But as I turn to you, you disappear—
And suddenly I know that I am growing old . . .

Then when I awoke
It felt like Russian winter;
Everything still cold and dark—
And I lay there helpless,
Like the Tolstoy hero
Knowing I was torn apart. . . .

From *Playboys of the Western World*:

"Never Stop"

Walls are what we build between us—
Words are what we use to screen us—
And so we live our lives—wanting love—
Until we stop (until we stop). . . .

Dreams are how we all perceive love—
Love is what we always dream of—
If not for all the fear—we feel inside—
That makes us stop (makes us stop)

Once in a while
A dream seems true
Until we wake to our fear

So we withdraw
Behind our walls—
Hoping for someone,
Dreaming of someone,
To help us to see
What we all need to see (You know)

Love is what we all believe in—
Even though it leaves some of us grieving—
So love me if you dare—but if you do—
You must never stop (never stop). . . .

From *At Our Sky-Blue Trade*:

"Angels, Angels . . ."

Angels, angels everywhere—
I hear them in the night;
The rustle of their satin wings
As they are taking flight. . . .

Angels, angels everywhere,
What message do they bring?
Have they come here to help me see—
Or just to hear me sing . . . ?

I do not understand.
Why would they come to me?
I am no great saint, you see—
And no great singer . . .

And when they have flown away,
I hear your voice, my love;
I call to you—but then
You do not answer. . . .

From *Once More into the Breach*:

"Anyone for Christmas?"

Angels and mangers and ivy and holly,
Bright-eyed children and Santa so jolly;
And you—what say you to . . .

Wishes for love and for joy and good cheer,
Bright stars and admonitions not to fear;
Anymore—so . . .

Anyone for Christmas?
Anyone for Christmas?
Anyone for peace and love and all that stuff?
God surely knows that we don't get enough
Through the year . . . so we need some . . .

Carols and sleigh bells and chestnuts and snow,
Fruitcakes and eggnog and green mistletoe;
So we're sure—that it's time to . . .

Send out a greeting to young and to old,
A merry song that might keep away cold
From the door—so . . .

Anyone for Christmas?
Anyone for Christmas?
Anyone for peace and love and all that stuff?
God surely knows that we don't get enough
Through the year . . . so we need some . . .

From ... *Nevermore.* ... :

"Circa 1976"

Hello there,
How are you doing?
Who is your friend?
Lovely to see you again ...
Oh, I'm fine now,
I'm writing songs
Between dates with the band—
See us whenever you can

This place looks like the last place;
This deal sounds like the last deal;
This one feels like the last one;
This song ends like the last song. ...

Hello, sir,
We're sending a song
That we'd like you to play—
We listen to you every day ...
It's different
And all of our friends, you know,
They like it well—
We think that it really could sell. ...

This place looks like the last place;
This deal sounds like the last deal;
This one feels like the last one;
This song ends like the last song. ...

Goodnight all,
We'd like to do one more

Before we must go—
Something to finish the show . . .
One last song—
Something to sing
As you're driving along—
Something you can take home . . .

This dive stinks like the last dive;
This jerk talks like the last jerk;
This drink tastes like the last drink;
This chick looks like the last chick;
This lie sounds like the last lie;
This hope fades like the last hope;
This dream dies like the last dream;
This song might be the last song. . . .

From *Lovely, Dark. and Deep*:

"Something Someone Said . . ."

Something happening here
That no one wants to talk about—
Except the usual complaints;
Someone doing wrong
Who doesn't want to take the blame—
Another sinner who is passing for a saint . . .

I saw a picture of my folks the other day
They were sitting on a tombstone,
They were smiling at the graves;
With all the love before them
To be won or lost—
They were so young then,
They couldn't know (they couldn't know) the cost. . . .

Something coming down
To which I simply can't respond—
I don't know what to feel;
Something understood
That I don't seem to understand—
I'm having trouble with determining what's real. . . .

I saw a picture of a child the other day
He was standing on the playground
As his friends all ran away
I thought I knew him
For a moment, then he changed
And he changed again (and changed again) until I
could not say . . .
Something going on

That I can't seem to figure out—
I can't add up the clues;
Something someone said
Who must've thought I couldn't hear
Another source who isn't giving me the news. . . .

I saw the cradle of my life the other day,
And my friends and family stood around it
Carefully arranged;
Why they were gathered
It was something someone said
But the who or what or why or how
Went right out of my head (my head, my head). . . .

(Really, Truly, Editor's Final Note: The major works, i.e. albums, are listed below. Singles are designated by asterisks. I've also included the unreleased ninth album that was to be called *Lovely, Dark, and Deep.* I can do this because I have a copy. Make friends with a few rock stars and you can get this kind of cool stuff. . . . As annotation, I offer what I thought was the best *and* worst thing I could find that a reviewer said about each album.)

The Lost Generation: A Discography

1. We Are All The Lost Generation (Released 12/74)

1) Falling in Love
2) Rebecca
3) Sweet Dreams*
4) I Still Love You
5) Go Now (à la the Moody Blues)
6) Her Smile, Winter 1974*
7) Mary, Quite Contrary*
8) Elizabethan Song*
9) Riding a Letter
10) Used to Dream About You
11) You Can Jump
12) Boys With Guitars and Dreams*

*Best thing a reviewer said: "The genre of rock called 'power pop' has a terrific new contender to pick up the mantle of Badfinger and The Raspberries." *The Sarasota Herald-Tribune*, **Jan. 25, 1975**

*Worst thing a reviewer said: "Someone should tell these 'Southern-fried Beatles' that 1966 is history." *Creem*, **Mar. 1975**

2. How Do You Like Your Blue-Eyed Boys? (Released 2/76)

1) River Kisses*
2) Conjunctive Adverb Blues
3) Just a Rainbow
4) True Love Comes Once
5) Jennifer on the Stairs
6) She's a Runaway
7) Masquerade for Two*
8) Somebody's Gone*
9) Say Goodbye to Sally
10) Return to Sender (à la Elvis)
11) Staying Up Again . . . *
12) Bird on the Wing

*Best thing a reviewer said: "With this second album, the band proves that maybe power pop should stay around." *Rolling Stone*, **Feb. 26, 1976**

*Worst thing a reviewer said: "Maybe if these guys wrote one song that actually *rocked* I could take them seriously, but all this preening and jangling while mewling and puking about chicks causes me to want to do a lot of the latter when I listen to them." *Circus*, **Mar. 1976**

3. Anthems for Doomed Youth (Released 8/77)

1) Leaves Like Love on Fire*
2) Loss of Control*
3) Renascence
4) Nothing Sacred*
5) Childe Harold
6) And if We Kiss . . .
7) Normal but Helpless
8) Can't Be Helped
9) Shapes of Things (à la The Yardbirds)
10) Pennsylvania
11) Car Won't Run
12) The Rock-and-Roll Ideal*

*Best thing a reviewer said: "For those for whom Led Zeppelin's bombast is too much for the psyche (not to mention the eardrums), The Lost Generation's new album offers gorgeous pop with chiming guitars and lovely tenor voices done by guys who look like the kind you wish Elaine would lead over to your table during a crowded lunch hour to ask if they could join you. . . ." *The New Yorker*, Aug. 29, 1977

*Worst thing a reviewer said: "When guys who provide music for college girls to masturbate to try to get serious, the results are about what you'd expect." *Creem*, Sept. 1977

4. War and Peace and Boredom (Released 11/78)

1) Fascination*
2) Pretend for a Minute
3) Disillusionment
4) I Don't Mind at All
5) Mick Doesn't Like This One
6) Like Russian Winter*
7) Many Days*
8) Not Like You
9) How Can I Win Your Love?*
10) Too Many Women Blues
11) Pictures of Lily (à la The Who)
12) Sometimes . . . *

*Best thing a reviewer said: "I *hate* power pop and I cannot stop listening to this album. Maybe being a Romantic is the way to go." *Rolling Stone*, Nov. 30, 1978

*Worst thing a reviewer said: "There comes a time when a style starts to become a formula. Sadly, for The Lost Generation, this album may be proof that they have moved to the formula stage of their careers." *Time*, Dec. 11, 1978

5. Playboys of the Western World (Released 3/80)

1) Salad Days*
2) No End
3) Clever As She Is
4) Never Stop*
5) Next Time
6) It's Your Birthday*
7) I Want You Back*
8) Le Roi Soleil
9) Eight Days a Week (à la The Beatles)
10) Monte Carlo Kay
11) Every Time
12) Rock-and-Roll Heroes

*Best thing a reviewer said: "Sometimes we hear it said that the proof of someone's ability is that he makes the difficult seem easy. Every artist and group should listen to this album to hear the proof of that claim." *New Music Express*, **Mar. 28, 1980**

*Worst thing a reviewer said: "This record proves that as long as these guys get to make records, the British Invasion will not be over." *Circus*, **Apr. 1980**

6. At Our Sky-Blue Trade (Released 4/82)

1) Love Me or Don't
2) Not like 17 (Kery's Song)*
3) Jewel-Eyed Judy (à la Fleetwood Mac)*
4) If She Sets Her Heart
5) Tomorrow
6) Could Be Anyone*
7) Rainbow Anyway
8) Chances
9) Oh, Her . . .
10) If This, Then That
11) Some Smiles
12) Angels, Angels . . . *

*Best thing a reviewer said: "Musical trends come and go in rock, but these fellows just keep pouring out beautiful power pop album after album." *Newsweek*, **Apr. 19, 1982**

*Worst thing a reviewer said: "They write beautiful songs, which they play beautifully and sing beautifully. They suck, nevertheless. . . ." *Kerrang!*, **May 3, 1982**

7. Once More into the Breach (Released 11/83)

1) The Moon Is Blue*
2) It's Been a Long, Long Time
3) I Guess You Never Really Know*
4) Keep Your Own Heart
5) Adieu, Rock-and-Roll
6) The Sailor Boy's Tale*
7) Buffalo Bill's . . .
8) Rock-and-Roll Woman (à la Buffalo Springfield)
9) Waiting for Your Love
10) All My Friends Are Giving Up . . .
11) Anyone for Christmas?*

*Best thing a reviewer said: "The band that has clearly influenced the New Romantics, such as ABC and Spandau Ballet, offers us an album to satisfy that need in us for something sad and lovely." *Rolling Stone*, **Nov. 24, 1983**

*Worst thing a reviewer said: "More of the same from power pop's saddest little boys. I guess dating fashion models and being pals with Calvin Klein and Ralph Lauren *are* **something to cry about."** *Hit Parader*, **April 1983**

8. . . . Nevermore. . . . (Released 9/85)

1) Circa 1976*
2) So You Say
3) The Wind Is My Lover
4) This Is How Lonely Feels
5) Lawyers*
6) What Does That Mean?
7) Too Rich, Too Thin . . . *
8) Sunny Afternoon (à la The Kinks)
9) Find Your Own Yoko
10) . . . Nevermore. . . .

*Best thing a reviewer said: "The Lost Generation has announced their break up. This last album, *Nevermore*, provides a sometimes-lovely ('So You Say'), sometimes-sad ('This is How Lonely Feels'), sometimes-wry ('Find Your Own Yoko') coda—after listening, it seems right to quote one of their earlier song titles, 'Adieu, Rock-and-Roll.'" *Rolling Stone*, Sept. 26, 1985

*Worst thing a reviewer said: "The Lost Generation calls it quits. 1967 rejoices as it can finally stop being relived and take its rightful place as history. Nevermore—we can only hope so." *Circus*, Oct. 1985

9. Lovely, Dark, and Deep (Recorded 1991–92; *Update*: Released 11/93)

1) Something Someone Said . . .
2) Hazy Ladies
3) Sun and Moon
4) Living With a Child's Faith
5) Time Plays Tricks
6) Looking Through Your Eyes
7) A Very Lovely Girl
8) I Don't Mind at All (live acoustic)
9) Best of Me
10) She's My Ooh La La
11) 3 Chords
12) Factory Girl (à la The Rolling Stones)

*Best thing a reviewer said: "In some ways they were marvels, in some ways, anomalies; in some ways, visionaries. As this long-rumored 'real final album' proves, they were what every rock band hopes to be—damned great at what they did." *Rolling Stone*, Nov. 25, 1993

*Worst thing a reviewer said: "Every successful rock band's career follows the same arc—they are discovered by rock's cognoscenti, they rise into the public consciousness, they trail across the sky for a few years, more comets than stars, then they descend below *our* horizon—and we await news: of glorious comeback, tragic, wasteful death, or something amusing such as a member breaking into a rich neighbor's home

while drink- or drug-addled. Sometimes they leave an artifact of one or the other of these fates. *Lovely, Dark, and Deep* is such an artifact. Of which of these fates it *is* an artifact is difficult to decide. . . ." *The New York Times,* Nov. 28, 1993

Epitaphs

"How refreshing the whinny of a packhorse unloaded
of everything!"
—Zen Saying

"Everything the same; everything distinct."
—Zen Proverb

"But these memories lose their meaning. . . ."
—Lennon/McCartney

"All in all I'd have to say . . ."
—Hatter/Breeze

ACKNOWLEDGEMENTS

I have resisted writing this acknowledgements page—
not from lack of need to acknowledge those many to
whom I owe much, but from fear that I will not
acknowledge everyone who deserves my thanks. This
book has taken far longer for me to write than I
meant it to, and many kind souls have contributed
ideas, reactions, and input.

First let me thank some fellow writers: Sam Smith
and Josh Booth, who have seen the manuscript in
various stages of readiness and have helped me
continue the work; Sam, Denny Wilkins, Brian
Angliss, Mike Sheehan, and all the wonderful writers
at the blog *Scholars and Rogues* who keep me on my
toes and make me be a better writer when I think I
can't do it.

Then there are some literary journals (and a couple of
editors) to thank: *The Dead Mule School of Southern
Literature* (and editor extraordinaire Val Macewan);
storySouth (and writer/editor Jason Sanford); and
other journals such as *Wilmington Blues* and *Pig Iron
Malt*.

Then there is my editor, Erin McKnight, and all the
good folks at Queen's Ferry Press who have guided me
through the process of book acceptance/editing/
preparation more thoughtfully and gracefully than I
could have thought possible.

Then there are the musicians who inspire me: some,

like Don Dixon, Jeffrey Dean Foster, Britt Uzzell, and Steve Caraway I'm lucky enough to know, some, like the guys in Doco (Josh and Trevor) I'm lucky enough to be related to, and some—many, many—whom I'll represent with four (for this guy) immortal names: John, Paul, George, and Ringo—are so much a part of my history that they're probably in my DNA.

Finally, there's Lovey—my wife, the artist Lea Booth, who inspires me with her talent and passion and who gets me to get things done—like this novel, for instance.

I know I've left someone out and I feel terrible.

Jim Booth is a fiction writer with over twenty-five published stories in journals ranging from *StorySouth* to *Dead Mule* to *Pig Iron Malt* to *Dew on the Kudzu*, and the author of *The New Southern Gentleman* (Wexford College Press, 2002) and *Morte D'Eden, or Tom Sawyer Meets the Rolling Stones* (Beach House Books, 2003).

Jim is fiction editor for *Scholars and Rogues Literary Magazine*, the literary arm of the national blog *Scholars and Rogues*.

A former touring rock musician, Jim currently operates his own independent record label, Goat Boy Records, and his sons Joshua and Trevor lead the rock group DoCo, currently on tour. Jim's wife Carolyn Lea Booth is an artist and poet whose work shows regularly in galleries in North Carolina and the Southeast.

CPSIA information can be obtained at www.ICGtesting.com
Printed in the USA
LVOW040204140812

294080LV00004BA/6/P